W9-ADP-199

Dead Clever

Also by Roderic Jeffries:

Death Trick
Relatively Dangerous
Almost Murder
Layers of Deceit
Three and One Make Five
Deadly Petard
Unseemly End
Just Deserts
Murder Begets Murder
Troubled Deaths

RODERIC JEFFRIES

Dead Clever

M

An Inspector Alvarez novel

St. Martin's Press
New York

 For information, address St. Martin's Press, 175 Fifth Avenue, New York, N.Y. 10010.

Library of Congress Cataloging-in-Publication Data

Jeffries, Roderic.
Dead clever / Roderic Jeffries.
p. cm.
ISBN 0-312-02899-7
I. Title.
PR6060.E43D39 1989
823'.914—dc19 89-4097
CIP

First published in Great Britain by William Collins Sons & Co., Ltd.

First U.S. Edition

10 9 8 7 6 5 4 3 2 1

Dead Clever

CHAPTER 1

The sun had warmed the sand until it was briefly uncomfortable to the touch; the sea was a deep, brilliant blue and flat calm, its surface disturbed only by the swimmers and the creaming wakes of power boats trailing skiers; across the bay, a thin column of smoke rose languidly from half way up the side of a mountain to mark a small bush fire.

To their right was the ferry landing-stage, where passengers from Puerto Llueso disembarked and embarked; to their left, beyond a line of Tahitian straw shades, was the much smaller landing-stage which belonged to the Parelona Hotel and off which were anchored two yachts and three power boats, all large and luxurious.

'Enrique, will you have some more tortilla?' asked Dolores.

Alvarez, his mouth full, shook his head.

'You don't like it?'

Hastily he swallowed, then said: 'It's delicious, but you gave me so much . . .'

'Nonsense! You'll have another slice.' She sat in the middle of the rug, in the shade of one of the pine trees which fringed the sand, and set out around her was so much food that she might have been catering for fifteen people, not five. She picked up a knife and prepared to cut the thick spanish omelette, made with eggs, potatoes, onions, peas, and peppers.

He said: 'That's a little too much . . .' He stopped because it was obvious she was ignoring him. Meekly he held out his plate for her to put the large slice on it. She was always inclined to be tetchy on a picnic and a wise man did nothing that might annoy her; in any case, it was a delicious omelette. He reached across for the bottle of wine and refilled his tumbler, then passed the bottle to Jaime. Jaime sneaked a quick glance at his wife and was delighted to note that she was not watching him; careless as to the reason for his good luck, he filled his glass to the brim.

Although she would never have admitted it, Dolores invariably felt ill at ease on the beach. The trouble was that Juan and Isabel demanded she went into the sea with them and this meant that she had to wear a bathing suit; she could never forget the teachings of her youth that it was immoral to expose a millimetre more of her body than was absolutely necessary to the gaze of any man other than her husband. Despite the fact that in her old-fashioned one-piece costume she was in comparison to most other women on the beach over-dressed, she still felt far too self-conscious to remember to check how much Jaime was drinking.

Alvarez finished eating and put the plate down on the rug. He belched quietly, drained his glass.

'You'll have some cake,' she said. It was a statement, not a question.

'I'd love some in a minute, but I've really eaten so much . . .'

'I made it because it's your favourite.'

'Then can I have some now? There's no one who can make a chocolate almond cake as well as you.'

She nodded because that was true. She opened a large tin and lifted out the cake which was topped with whipped cream. She cut a very large slice, put this on a plate, passed the plate to him.

He had not finished eating when Juan and Isabel left the sea and wove their way between sunbathers and up the beach to the rug. 'I'm starving,' Juan announced. 'Is that chocolate almond cake that Uncle's eating? I want some.'

Dolores spoke severely. 'Ask politely or you'll go on wanting.'

'He's rude,' said Isabel.

'I'm not,' retorted Juan.

'You told me that very rude word just now.'

'No, I didn't,' he denied unconvincingly.

'And you saw those rude people.'

'Everyone saw them. You saw them, didn't you?'

'But you did first.'

'Can't you two ever stop bickering?' asked Jaime. 'What are you on about now?'

The children looked at each other, giggled.

Dolores said: 'Why are you being so stupid?'

Isabel, between giggles, answered. 'We saw some rude ladies. They weren't wearing any costumes at all.'

'Don't be ridiculous!'

'It's true,' said Juan. 'We could see their—'

'Be quiet! If there's any more of this, as soon as we get home I'll wash your mouths out with soap.' She noticed that Jaime was staring along the beach in the direction from which the children had come. 'You are staying right here.'

Jaime felt aggrieved. His intentions had not been prurient. He had not lusted after the sight of naked women, but surely someone should check whether the children were telling the truth since if they were, then it was manifestly wrong to accuse them of lying . . .

They arrived home just after five. Alvarez was hanging up the towels and costumes in the enclosed patio beyond the kitchen, so hot and airless that he was sweating heavily, when he heard the telephone ring. A moment later, Dolores shouted out that the call was for him.

When he entered the kitchen, she was unpacking one of the two chilled picnic boxes. 'Who's calling?'

'Palma,' she answered, as she carried some wrapped sliced ham over to the refrigerator.

'But who in Palma?'

'How should I know?' She shut the refrigerator door and

returned to the table. 'All they said was that they wanted you. I'm not a mind-reader.'

He wondered how many times he'd asked her always to learn the name of a caller? The telephone was in the front room, furnished as a sitting-room which was used only on formal occasions. A woman who sounded as if she'd a plum in her mouth said that Superior Chief Salas wanted to speak to him. He waited, certain that he did not want to speak to his superior chief.

'Where the devil have you been all day?'

It was so typical of a Madrileño to speak with such abrupt discourtesy. 'How do you mean, señor?'

'I mean I've been trying to get hold of you for hours, but you weren't in your office and no one at the post had the slightest idea where you were. What's been going on?'

Knowing that Salas was a very impatient man, and needing to divert him from any more embarrassing questions, Alvarez began a long and deliberately rambling explanation. 'I've been making inquiries, following a tip-off. There's this man who lives in the port and whose father was wounded in the war and was refused a pension because he fought for the other side and he—that is, the son—has to—'

'Surely you're aware that standing orders dictate that at all times the duty officer must be informed of your whereabouts?'

'Indeed, señor, and naturally I normally make absolutely certain that he knows exactly where I am. But that just wasn't possible in this case because I had to move so quickly. You see, the son only gave me the information rather late. It wasn't his fault. He's a very good informer. People think he's a little simple and so they speak freely in front of him, but he's not so simple that he doesn't understand what they're saying. As his mother said to me once, "Victoriano is a lot smarter than he looks." Of course, that is not so very difficult—'

'Alvarez, do you imagine I've nothing better to do than to listen to you waffling on and on?'

'No, señor. I know that you are a very busy man indeed—'

'Then listen. I've received a request from the British Embassy in Madrid, passed through the Ministry. They are asking us to provide assistance to an investigator who is coming from England. Since you speak English, it will have to be you. Do you understand?'

'Not really, señor—'

'I will explain in simpler terms. An Englishman arrives on the island tomorrow and it will be your duty to assist him in any reasonable way that you can.'

'I presume he's a policeman?'

'You presume incorrectly.'

'Then who is he?'

'He works for an insurance company. I naturally made the point that we of the Cuerpo General de Policia should not be expected to concern ourselves with helping a foreign civilian, but my objection was overruled. Just one more consequence of the stupidity of our politicians in joining the Common Market.'

'What is the problem?'

'If you can't see that to give up sovereignty is to deal a foul blow to the pride of every Spaniard—'

Alvarez risked a quick correction. 'I really meant, señor, what is the problem which brings the Englishman to the island?'

'All the man to whom I spoke could tell me was that the Englishman wishes to make some inquiries concerning the recent air disaster . . . Are you aware of the fact that a light aircraft took off from the old airport and crashed into the sea?'

'Yes, señor. Why is the Englishman interested in the crashed plane?'

'I was not informed.'

'Then I wonder if—'

'Perhaps for once you will eschew all surmises and wait to learn the facts before expressing an opinion?'

'Yes, señor.'

'And one last thing. You will not, I repeat not, complicate what must in essence undoubtedly be a simple and straightforward matter.'

'Señor, it has never been I who has complicated events, it has always been the facts—' He did not have a chance to finish; the connection was cut.

He replaced the receiver. He yawned. It had been a very tiring afternoon because Isabel and Juan had badgered him into helping them build sandcastles and he'd had to forgo a siesta. He yawned again. Undoubtedly, even a brief nap would refresh him and enable him to do his work much better.

He was half way up the stairs when it occurred to him that Salas had not told him either the name of the Englishman or the other's time of arrival. He shrugged his shoulders. There was plenty of time in which to find out the details.

CHAPTER 2

The sky was just beginning to darken in the east as Alvarez entered Terminal B at Son San Juan airport. He crossed to look at the indicator for foreign arrivals. Despite the fact that the Gatwick plane had been due to land ten minutes previously, and an earlier telephone call had determined that there were no delays, there was no green light or landing tab to say that it had arrived. He walked through the hall to the main information desk where a woman in Iberia uniform was having a long and intimate telephone conversation with a friend. Eventually, she replaced the receiver and irritatedly asked him what he wanted. After consulting the VDU, she said that the plane had landed fifteen minutes previously.

He returned to the arrival hall and, after identifying himself to the police, passed through the doorway. Inside there was turmoil since four flights had arrived in quick succession and as yet none of the luggage had been unloaded from the planes because the porters hadn't finished their coffee-break. Clearly there was no chance of his identifying Ware on sight, so he spoke to the sargento at one of the desks and asked him to page Señor Robert Ware on the PA system.

Ware proved to be several inches taller than Alvarez—and several inches slimmer. Dressed casually, but neatly, in a lightweight sports jacket, open neck shirt, and blue cotton trousers, his face was brown, in contrast to the whiteness of so many of his fellow passengers, and strongly featured; there were lines of humour about his mouth. He looked, decided Alvarez, to be the kind of person all Englishmen had been presumed to be before package holidays brought too many to the island for any generalization to remain valid.

'Señor Ware, I am Inspector Enrique Alvarez of the Cuerpo General de Policia. Superior Chief Salas asked me to welcome you to Mallorca and to say that I shall be happy to offer you all possible assistance.'

'Great! And even greater to discover that you speak English like a native.' His cheerful grin reached round his face. 'Since I was assigned to this job, I've been swotting up on a Spanish phrase book—and coming to the conclusion that I'll starve because I'll never remember anything and no one will understand what I'm saying even if I do . . . By the way, the name's Robert or Bob; but if it's all the same to you, not Bobby because for some reason that name makes me cringe.'

'I will try to remember that.'

There was a swirling movement among part of the crowd

and Ware looked across to see that one of the indicators at the head of a carousel was now showing his flight. 'It looks as if the luggage has finally started to come through so I'll go over and collect my bag.'

'First tell me, do you have a hotel reservation? If not, I will arrange a room while you claim your luggage. It is not easy to get a good room at this time of the year, you'll understand, but I do have friends in the business who owe me favours . . .'

'That's very kind of you, but I booked by phone last night. I'm staying at the Vefour.'

'The Vefour?' said Alvarez curiously. 'I don't think I know it.'

'It's a small place up in the hills where my wife and I stayed a few years back. We both thought it as close to heaven as we'd ever be allowed to climb. They say never go back to somewhere you've once loved, but I decided to take the risk. Not that I had the courage to tell her!'

Since tourism had revolutionized the entire economy of the island, it was ridiculous to suggest that anywhere or anything had remained unchanged; even the farmer from the mountains who had once been faced with a day-long mule-cart ride to the nearest shop now made the journey by car in half an hour and once there was faced with a bewildering choice of goods for sale. But the Vefour still possessed unmistakable links with the days when Mallorca was truly the Island of Calm, each village regarded the next village as foreign land, and the people's standards were those of honesty and compassion because none of them had been corrupted by a flood of foreign money or bewildered by foreign sophistication.

The hotel lay half way up a hill, on a shelf of land little more than half a hectare in size. Originally a typical Mallorquin farmhouse, built in stone to the simplest possible design, it had been enlarged and modernized, but in character so that it still looked almost part of the rocky soil on which it stood. It was owned by a family who had had the wit to perceive that there would always be a few people who preferred quiet simplicity to raucous sophistication; although each bedroom had its own shower, there was no chromium bar, no piped music, no television room, no sauna, and discothèque was a dirty word—it had been years before the swimming-pool had been built; service was friendly, but if one liked to be treated with servility because one tipped well, one left and went elsewhere; several tour operators had wanted to include the hotel in their up-market holidays, but all had been politely turned down.

In the summer, guests could if they wished dine outside; most so wished. At night, while the whole of the bay was visible, Palma became merely an attractive jumble of lights and one could forget how much of the shoreline had been ruined by development. Few cars used the road and for most of the time one could hear the shrilling of cicadas, the belling of Scops Owls, and the croaking of nightjars.

The waiter—he was one of the sons and very like his father in appearance—put the two Martinis on the table, wished them good drinking, and left. Ware raised his glass. 'To a life where time stands still.'

Alvarez drank. 'It sounds as if things here are very much as you remember them?'

'Exactly. And I'll swear that none of the family is a day older. I wouldn't be at all surprised if they all live to be centenarians, like those people in Georgia.' He stared out at the distant bay for several seconds, then sighed. 'If only time really could stand still when one wants it to, and not when one doesn't . . . You said you know hardly any of the details of the case?'

'It would be more accurate to say that I know none of them; that is, apart from the fact that a small plane flew from this island and disappeared into the sea.'

'Then I'll set the scene. I'm what's called a loss adjuster, which means I'm called in when a claim is made against an insurance company and they have their doubts about the genuineness of the claim; it's my job to find out if their doubts are justified. Almost certainly, you have the same kind of set-up here?'

'Indeed, but not for very long since it is only recently that the ordinary person has owned anything worth insuring.' Alvarez chuckled. 'And now when we wish to describe someone who is really simple, we say that he is a man who forgets to check that his insurance is up to date before he sets fire to his house.'

The waiter brought their first course—sopas Mallorquinas for Alvarez and grilled gambas for Ware.

'I've been dreaming of these,' said Ware, as he picked up the first of the six very large prawns. He pulled the head away, stripped off the legs and shell, popped the meat into his mouth. 'As delicious as I've been imagining, so don't ever tell me that dreams don't come true. I daren't tell Heather I've had these or she'll divorce me for cruelty . . . To return to essentials. The twin-engined Flèche which flew from this island and crashed into the sea was piloted by a man called Timothy Green who had a life policy with the Crown and Life Insurance Company; it's they who've called me in.

'The policy was first taken out just about three years ago and Green declared, as bound to do, that he held a pilot's licence and from time to time flew himself about the world. Obviously, the premium charged took account of this additional risk and the policy contained the standard clause that it would only be valid if, in the event of any accident while piloting an aircraft, he held a current licence.'

Ware was silent as he ate a couple more prawns. Noticing that Alvarez's glass was almost empty, he refilled it, and his own, from the bottle of Bach. 'At the end of the first year, Green asked that the capital sum assured be increased by roughly the rate at which inflation was running. Since this was no more than prudent financial management on his part, the increase was granted without any further questions. The same thing happened at the end of the second year. Then, just over a fortnight ago—which is a few weeks short of when, if the sequence had been observed, Green would have been making another application to raise the sum assured by the rate of inflation—he telephoned to say that he wanted to double the amount. Naturally, a rise of this magnitude—and we're now talking about half a million —wasn't automatically granted and he was referred to a senior employee who tactfully explained that when so large an increase was sought, it was company practice to ask the policy holder to come to the office for a chat and possibly to undergo a fresh medical check—in other words, the company wanted to judge whether everything was still in order. Green claimed this was impossible because of his business commitments which included an imminent trip abroad, but that he had to have the increased insurance because he was soon marrying again and he wanted to be certain that his wife would be financially secure if anything unfortunate happened to him. The manager was sympathetic but inflexible; until Green came to the office and talked things over, nothing more could be done. Green began to argue and, according to the manager, became obnoxiously abusive.'

Ware refilled their glasses. 'Drink up so that we can kill this bottle and have another.' He smiled. 'Ordering a second bottle of wine without nervously consulting my wallet always convinces me I really am in Spain!'

They finished their first course. As the waiter cleared the plates, Ware turned to Alvarez. 'D'you object to smoking between courses?'

'On the contrary.'

'A man after my own heart!' He brought a pack of cigarettes from his pocket and offered it. 'Heather says it's the sign of a barbarian. So, I tell her, I'm a barbarian.' He flicked open a lighter and then, when their cigarettes were alight, settled back in his chair. 'In the light of what I've told you, you won't be surprised to learn that when the company received the report that an aircraft, piloted by Green, had disappeared into the sea, they immediately began to ask questions. Which is why I'm here now.'

'They think it might have been a faked accident?'

'In one. And not just because, without the increase asked for, the sum involved is in the order of a quarter of a million; after all, when businessmen are vain enough to value their lives in millions, that isn't very much. It's because of the pattern. As you suggested earlier, taking an insurance company on a faked claim has been popular ever since insurance was invented. But criminals aren't usually all that imaginative and their methods of fraud tend to run in patterns. Obviously, a man who takes out an insurance today and claims on it tomorrow is going to be suspected, so the fraudster tries to establish himself as honest and the most popular way of doing this is to work to a distant dateline and for a while to pay the premiums on the dot and to increase the sum insured by only a reasonable amount, which is to say by no more than would a prudent man who'd never thought of swindling anyone in the whole of his life. Then, when satisfied he's established himself, he produces a good reason for asking the capital sum assured to be increased considerably and after another pause he fakes his own death.'

Alvarez spoke diffidently, rather afraid that what he said might appear to be reflecting on Ware's ability as an insurance investigator. 'If this were the pattern that Green were following, wouldn't he have waited to fake his own death until the sum assured had been increased and he would judge enough time had passed after that for suspicions to be dulled?'

'Normally, the answer has to be yes. But it's more than

possible that he suddenly discovered he didn't have all the time available that he'd been banking on and so if he was to carry out the fraud at all, he had to do it quickly. I know that if one were in his position and looked at the facts logically, one would say that it must be too dangerous to act precipitately and the idea must be dropped, but a criminal who's spent a lot of thought and time on a projected job often can't view it logically; and as you'll know much better than I, fraudsters tend to be at the smart end of the criminal tree and it's my experience that a smart man can get so puffed up with pride in his own smartness that he behaves like a plain, ordinary fool.'

'That can be very true.' Alvarez fiddled with some crumbs from his roll, kneading them into a pellet. 'But from what you say you cannot as yet be certain that the crash was faked?'

'That's right. Which is why I'd be grateful for all the help you can give me.'

'Of course.'

'Starting off by seeing the officials at the airport who'll be able to provide us with a much more detailed account of events than I have at the moment.'

'I'll ring them first thing tomorrow and find out exactly who to talk to and then arrange a meeting.'

'That's great!' Ware drained his glass. 'Where's that other bottle? . . . You know, Enrique, sitting out here under the stars, eating ambrosia and drinking nectar, I realize I'm a prime candidate for the deadly sin of gluttony!'

CHAPTER 3

A sound disturbed Alvarez's sleep and he opened his eyes and stared at the far wall of the bedroom, clearly visible although both shutters and curtains were closed. He vaguely wondered what the sound could have been as he languidly and pleasurably drifted back to sleep . . .

There was a pounding on the bedroom door which startled him fully awake. 'Are you deaf?' Dolores called out.

'What's the matter?' he asked thickly, confusedly wondering if catastrophe had overtaken them all.

'I've called you twice already. Aren't you working today?'

'Of course I am.'

'Then you'd best get up before it's time to start tomorrow.'

After a while he reluctantly climbed out of bed, crossed to the window, drew the curtains, unclipped and opened the shutters. Sharp sunshine engulfed him and he felt the heat on his bare chest. He stared over the rooftops of the village houses at Puig Antonia. The buildings on the top of the sugar-loaf mountain had originally been a hermitage, but now nuns from a contemplative order lived in them. Hermitages in many parts of the island had fallen into desuetude, as hermitages, at around the time when the tourist industry had begun to bring prosperity. Presumably it was easier to renounce the material world when that offered little to be renounced . . .

Dolores called from the foot of the stairs: 'If you're not down inside five minutes, you'll have to get your own chocolate.'

'I'm just coming.' Dolores, he thought as he began to dress, was becoming sharper with every day. Jaime should have read her the riot act a long time ago. Threatening to leave the house before she had prepared his breakfast!

She spoke even more aggressively when he entered the kitchen. 'You know why you couldn't get up when you should, don't you? You drank too much last night.'

'I did not.'

'Then why were you snoring so loudly in the middle of the night that you woke me up?'

'Because you're a light sleeper. In any case, snoring has

nothing to do with drinking . . . And if you must know, I had dinner with an English señor who would never drink too much and all we had was a little wine. After we'd finished the meal, I came straight home.'

'I doubt very much it was straight.' She carried a mug of hot chocolate over to the table and put it down in front of him. 'I'm off now. You'll be the last to leave the house, so don't forget to lock up.'

'Just before you go, where's the coca?'

Her tone was scornful. 'You think I have the time to make a coca for a man who demands his breakfast when it's almost lunch-time? . . . If you want something to eat, there's bread in the bin.' She walked out of the kitchen with her head held high, her expression one of haughty disdain.

He drank some of the chocolate, then went through to the dining-room and across to the large and ornately carved cupboard from which he brought out a bottle which he used to top up the chocolate with brandy. Breakfast was an important meal for a busy man.

Alvarez and Ware met at the airport, outside the new control tower. The guard on the main entrance directed them over to a lift and this took them to the lower of two floors which were immediately below the main control area. There was a central, octagonally shaped lobby and off this radiated offices. They entered the one on the door of which was printed 'Co-ordinator'.

Murillo was only in his middle forties, but a receding hairline and a heavily lined face, in which one eyelid drooped, made him look considerably older. He shook hands briefly, as if he found prolonged physical contact distasteful, returned to his seat behind a large and rather ugly desk. The roar of a jet caused him to look through the large window and he watched an Aviaco 727 climb, leaving a dirty trail of exhaust smoke, then he turned back and said:

'How can I help you, Inspector?' Both his tone and manner asked them to be as brief as possible.

'Señor Ware has come from England to make inquiries about the crash last Saturday night.'

'So I understood from your telephone call.'

'He'd be most grateful if now you'd give him all the known facts regarding that crash.'

Murillo nodded, turned over some papers on his desk and found the one he wanted, read quickly, then said, clipping his words short: 'The plane was a twin-engined, turbo-prop Flèche with long-range fuel tanks. It arrived at fourteen thirty-five on the Thursday, landing at the old airport. Green, the pilot and only occupant, cleared customs and immigration very soon afterwards.' He waited, impatiently, while Alvarez translated.

'On the Friday—in accordance with regulations—he gave notice of his intention to fly off on Saturday evening and he handed in his flight plan and asked for refuelling the next day. His declared destination, Shoreham, meant a flying time which came a long way inside the period before the next engine service was due.

'At twenty-one hundred hours, on Saturday, he reported to customs and emigration and received a meteorological and flight briefing. He checked that the plane had been refuelled and paid the account.

'He took off at twenty-two thirty-five. Conditions were good—winds southerly, force three, eight-tenths cloud, excellent visibility, and no change expected. Ground staff confirm that on take-off both engines were working perfectly. Radar noted that he kept to his route.

'At twenty-two fifty-five, he sent out a mayday. He reported that his starboard engine had suddenly died and his port one was misfiring and he was turning back. Two minutes later he said that the misfiring on the port engine was becoming worse; after this, radio contact was lost. Radar showed the plane descending gradually, then abruptly plummeting. The image was lost twelve minutes after the last radio contact, when the plane was at roughly two hundred metres height.

'Rescue services were alerted and a full search was mounted and this continued throughout the night; at midday on Sunday the air search was called off and at dark, the sea search. No sign of wreckage was found . . . That is everything.'

After Alvarez finished translating, Ware looked up from his notebook. 'Radar lost the plane at two hundred metres —why's that?'

'The radar set on the mountains cannot track below that height above sea level.'

'Then is it possible that the plane could have dropped below the two hundred metres, levelled out, and continued on its way?'

'In the dark, señor, no pilot would be so foolhardy as to try to fly that low.'

'Not if he'd some pressing reason for doing so? And since the sky was two-tenths clear, there must have been a certain amount of moonlight to mark the sea.'

Murillo tried not to speak too scathingly. 'It would seem, señor, that you do not know too much about flying?'

'Change that to nothing,' replied Ware cheerfully.

'Then permit me to explain something. Moonlight and the sea form a deadly combination which can render a man's judgement of height useless. He may think he's a hundred metres above the water, but in truth he may well be skimming it so that if he loses only a few metres, he hits.'

'I can understand that, but sometimes a man's willing to take a risk that any sensible person would refuse. Do you know what sort of cloud cover there was at the time of the crash?'

'I will find out.' He used the internal phone to speak to a member of the meteorological office and after a longish wait, during which he drummed on the desk with his fingers, his query was answered. He replaced the receiver. 'The nearest time at which there was an observation was twenty-three hundred hours. Then, cloud coverage was still eight-tenths.'

'Presumably, that observation was taken here. Out at sea, there might have been more moonlight?'

Murillo gestured with his hands. 'Señor, that is so, but there is little relevance to the fact. As I said, radar contact was lost at about two hundred metres; it is estimated that at that point the plane was making around two hundred knots and so it is impossible that the pilot could have levelled out before the plane struck the sea.'

'Then there is no doubt that the plane did crash?'

'None whatsoever.'

Ware thought for a moment, then said: 'The plane had been properly serviced and its engines were sounding good when it took off, so is there any suggestion why one engine abruptly cut out and the other misfired badly?'

'No. There is no explanation.'

'Could the fuel have been the trouble?'

'We do not supply faulty fuel.'

Belatedly, Ware realized that while so direct a question was normal in Britain, it was not in Spain. 'Señor, I was not for a moment suggesting there could have been any inefficiency on the part of anyone here.'

Despite the fact that it was difficult to see how the question could escape such an implication, Murillo accepted the denial.

'Presumably, other planes have been refuelled from the same source since then?' Ware asked.

'And the fuel has proved to be faultless.'

'Then we've covered everything. Thank you for giving me so much of your valuable time.'

Ware was silent until they were in the lift and then, as Alvarez pressed the button for the ground floor, he said: 'That would seem to be that. The plane definitely crashed into the sea.'

'Certainly there can be no other conclusion.'

'So this is a claim that's genuine, despite the surrounding circumstances, and the company's going to have to pay.'

Alvarez telephoned Palma and asked the secretary with a plummy voice if Superior Chief Salas was in; to his regret, she said that he was.

'Señor, I have just returned from the airport with Señor Ware. From the inquiries we've made, it's clear that the Englishman, Green, was piloting the plane when it crashed into the sea.'

'Are you saying that you can be certain beyond any shadow of a doubt that the Englishman is dead?'

'Yes, señor.'

'Then undoubtedly he is alive and well,' said Salas bad temperedly before he replaced the receiver.

CHAPTER 4

Unless he considered that there were too many pressing cases in hand—and he seldom did—Alvarez did not work on Saturday afternoons. Man, he was fond of saying, could not live by work alone. He was seated at his desk late Saturday morning, contemplating the pleasures of the coming meal and the subsequent prolonged siesta, when the telephone rang. He wondered whether to ignore it, but there was always the chance that the caller was Salas who would be only too aware of the fact that the time was, as yet, not appropriate to having stopped work. He lifted the receiver.

'Enrique, I've some news that'll interest you!'

He recognized Ware's voice.

'I've just had a call from England to say that although

Timothy Green does not have a criminal record, he was once very close to being arrested for fraud.'

'I can see, of course, how that might have been important before we spoke to Señor Murillo, but surely now . . .?'

'I know what you're thinking. If he had had ten convictions for defrauding insurance companies it doesn't alter anything because his plane quite definitely crashed into the sea. But having learned his history, there's something I'd like to talk over with you and since I've never seen your end of the island, what say I hire a car and drive across and we can have dinner together at the restaurant of your choice and on my expense account?'

'That would be very pleasant. But I'm afraid I can't meet you until after six.'

'They're making you work over the weekend in weather like this? . . . Let's say half six, then. Where shall we meet?'

'How about the car park on the front down in the port?'

After ringing off, Alvarez locked the fingers of his hands together and rested them on his stomach. It was strange how northern Europeans had never discovered that the secret of a happy life lay not in pursuing the Holy Grail, but in not pursuing it.

As Alvarez parked, Ware came up to his car. 'I'm dying of thirst. What would you say to a drink before anything else?'

'I can't imagine anything better.' Alvarez climbed out of the car.

'Then let's walk along the front. There are several cafés with tables set outside and for me the epitome of life on the Continent is to sit at an outside table, watching the world go by.'

'The front cafés charge twice as much as the ones a road back.'

'The Crown and Life Insurance Company made a record profit last year; they can afford to treat us generously.'

They walked past the eastern arm of the harbour and

along the road, closed to traffic, until they reached the first café outside which were set a number of tables, each with a sun umbrella.

Ware sat, facing the bay. After a moment he said: 'The island must have been an absolute jewel before all the development started.'

'It was.'

'Who on earth was so blind as to allow so much of the coastline to be spoiled?'

'An envelope filled with pesetas makes most men blind.'

'I know. It's the same all over the world. And when I get too holier-than-thou about such things at home, Heather always asks me if I owned a piece of beauty which someone wanted to develop, would I keep on saying no however fat the envelope became. If I'm honest, I don't know the answer.'

The waiter came up to the table and they ordered drinks.

Ware offered cigarettes, then said: 'I wasn't surprised this morning when my news left you cold. But the thing is, I sometimes get a hunch that a claim is false and right from the start I've had a hunch that this one is. And on top of that, by now there are a lot of unanswered questions. Green hired a plane in England, flew here and was only here for a couple of days. Why go to all that very considerable expense when he wasn't a wealthy man and there are such good commercial air services? Why did he fly out after dark? If the engines of the plane were in good order—which they were—why should both give trouble when we can be reasonably certain that the fuel was OK? Is it chance that the plane crashed at sea and not on land, where the wreckage could have been found and his body examined?'

'But you agree that the plane did crash at sea?'

'Yes. What I'm saying now is, was Green in it when it crashed? . . . Suppose radio contact was lost because he wanted it to be and not because the emergency had overwhelmed him?'

'Were there parachutes aboard?'

'I'm not sure, but in any case he could have loaded a steerable one before he flew out of the UK.'

'But there was a full-scale search of the crash area and he was never sighted.'

The waiter brought the drinks. Ware raised his glass. 'If I said, the first today, I'd be a liar!' He drank. 'This afternoon I phoned a contact in the UK and talked to him about the twin-engined Flèche. He described it as a very well built plane with an impressive safety record and he's never heard of both engines failing. It has a cruising speed of a hundred and ninety knots—roughly two hundred and eighteen statute miles—and it's pressurized up to twenty thousand feet. Equipment includes the latest Nebacco auto-pilot which has three trim tabs and one on/off switch.

'Remember the sequence of events? Green leaves Palma and twenty minutes later sends out an SOS. He's now roughly seventy miles out from the island, so he turns back rather than trying to make the mainland. Two minutes later he sends a second message and after that there is silence. The plane crashes twelve minutes later or perhaps thirty-three miles out and naturally the search is carried out at this last position.

'Now assume that just before his first message he sights his rescue craft. He circles round, makes a second radio call, throttles back sufficiently to give a speed commensurate with a plane suffering engine trouble, sets the auto-pilot and activates a timer which in so many minutes will disengage it—this can either be a mechanical device attached to the on/off switch or a small explosive charge which will wreck everything. He jumps. The auto-pilot compensates for the sudden loss of weight and the plane flies on until the auto-pilot is disengaged and then, either quickly or after a while depending on air conditions, it crashes into the sea. The object of all this is, of course, to make certain that the rescue operations are concentrated well away—at least thirty miles—from the position where he jumped and was picked up.'

Alvarez spoke slowly. 'But if Green did jump . . .'

Ware interrupted him. 'Before you start listing objections, listen to a few facts which have been dug up in the UK. Four and a half years ago he had a very well paid job as a salesman with a finance company. He made a lot of money and spent it all. Then the company closed and he was out of a job. He found great trouble in obtaining a fresh one, despite the fact that he was reputed to have a golden tongue that could sell an oil well to the Sheikh of Dubai, and when he did he earned very much less than before. He found it impossible to live within his reduced income and amassed considerable debts. It seems—though this is as yet unsubstantiated—that he tried to bolster his finances by gambling, failed, and ended up owing a large sum of money, which he'd no hope of repaying, to a man who wouldn't hesitate to send out a squad of heavies to persuade him to find it from somewhere.

'He took up the sport of parachuting after his income was so severely reduced and soon became good enough to be a member of a club's competition team.

'His marriage went sour and he and his wife separated, although there hasn't been a divorce. She went to court and was awarded an allowance, but has had repeatedly to resort to solicitors to try to make him pay up.

'Finally, and most interestingly, the firm for which he worked until four years ago was owned by Patrick Bennett and it dealt in Over-the-Counter shares. Does that mean anything to you?'

'Not a thing.'

'Shares aren't my scene either, but I'll make things as clear as I can. In the UK we have three markets in shares, the third and lowest of which has been given the plebeian name of Over-the-Counter, or OTC. This means that dealers bring stocks to the market and make the market;

that is to say, if they are the only dealers handling a particular stock, they list the buy and sell price solely according to their own judgements and not because of market forces. Obviously, this can—and does—make for a very volatile market and a buyer can find himself in the position of wanting to sell stock back to the dealer and being quoted a price that must mean a very heavy loss, but being unable to avoid this because no one else will offer to buy the stock from him. By now you're probably beginning to wonder why anyone should be foolhardy enough to venture into a set-up which is tailor-made for suckering. The answer is twofold: first, because it is such a volatile market, it is possible—especially if one chooses stock which is handled by two or more dealers—to get the timing right and to make a great deal of money in a very short time; secondly, under a government scheme, rich men can invest in companies which are quoted in this market and, subject to certain conditions, can gain tax relief up to a considerable amount. If the stock gains, they're doing very nicely; if it loses, but by less than the tax relief is worth to them, they're still smiling.

'Which is where Bennett came in. He handled stock likely to attract rich men and for which he was the only dealer. He made the prices and naturally these fluctuated, but almost without exception when a holder came to sell the price was lower than when he'd bought; yet not so low that he showed an overall loss when the benefits of tax relief were taken into account. The stock Bennett had bought back at a low price could later be sold to a fresh buyer at a high price. It was a clever way of making money and it was perfectly legal, subject to one proviso—that it could not be proved that he was deliberately rigging the market in order to ensure that every punter suffered a loss. I don't need to point out to you that the only feasible way of proving such rigging would be to show that over a period he had knowingly bought high and sold low, not because of the way the market was moving, but in order to make the maximum amount of money for himself.

'Not surprisingly, his actions had come to the attention of the authorities and they'd considered whether he'd been guilty of, and could be charged with, criminal fraud, but it was finally and regretfully decided that it would be almost impossible to prove to the satisfaction of any court that he'd been pursuing a criminal course of action. Few would be prepared to testify against him—rich men don't like admitting that they've been suckered and if a rich man's loss is represented by a small overall gain, the ordinary man is going to find it difficult to believe that the rich man has been swindled. So Bennett escaped prosecution and retired a multi-millionaire, who will, one imagines, never invest in OTC stock. And, no doubt, revels in his life of luxury in Llueso.'

'You're saying that he lives here?' asked Alvarez, his voice high from surprise. 'Then Green . . .' He became silent.

'Was picked up by a boat skippered by Bennett.'

'Why should Bennett take such a risk?'

'Green had worked for him and therefore was in a position to provide the proof that he had been deliberately rigging the market.'

'Wouldn't it have made more sense for Green simply to blackmail him instead of going to all the trouble of setting up so elaborate an insurance swindle?'

'It might have done if Green hadn't had a wife who was pursuing him financially and a creditor who was threatening to put the heavies on him. He needed to disappear conclusively and this with sufficient funds to see him through the rest of his life. The insurance company would pay the money to his girlfriend, assuming she was sole beneficiary under his will, and the wife would have to go to court to establish any claim to it; obviously, a fruitless task.'

'You've made it all sound plausible.'

'Good. Then you'll agree that we need to talk to Bennett?'

'Of course.'

'Now?'

Alvarez shook his head. 'It's getting on; we can visit him tomorrow.'

Ware was about to argue, when he relaxed. 'Mañana. The Spanish gift to gracious living.' He drained his glass, signalled to a waiter, and ordered fresh drinks. Then he watched three young and shapely women lay out towels on the sand and strip off their bikini tops.

CHAPTER 5

As they braked to a stop it immediately became clear that here was no ordinary property. High and elaborate wrought-iron gates, electrically operated, hung from pillars of faced stone; set into the right-hand pillar was a speaker unit, below which was a notice in English, French, and Spanish, asking callers to press the red button; fixed to a nearby olive tree was a small, all-weather TV camera; a beautifully constructed drystone wall stretched away on either side of the gates to encircle the hill and curving round with the wall were cypresses; on the top of the hill stood a large house, immediately notable for the fact that, unlike almost all other houses on the island, its lines were graceful rather than square and boxy.

Alvarez left the car, crossed to the speaker unit, and pressed the red button. A woman, her voice made tinny by the speaker, asked him in Spanish what he wanted. He told her who he was and said he'd like a word with Señor Bennett, if at home.

'Yes, he's here. I'll open the gates.'

As he returned to the car, the gates opened; one of them briefly made a screeching noise which caused him to wince. Ware engaged first gear and drove forward.

As it rose, the road wound round the hill and it reached the top on the north side. Here there was a lawn, a turning circle enclosing a raised bed of roses, and several shaped flowerbeds all filled with colour. Alvarez stared at the scene with amazement, not because the formal lay-out was so alien to a Mediterranean island, but because he was certain that every litre of water used had to be trucked up and it was mind-boggling to estimate what that must cost in the height of the summer.

There was a portico and the front door was made from a dark, beautifully grained wood panelled in traditional style. A middle-aged woman, dressed in a maid's frock, escorted them through an air-conditioned, high-ceilinged hall and very large sitting-room—overburdened with antique furniture, carpets, paintings, and display cabinets—out to the patio. Beyond the patio was a lawn—larger than the one at the front of the house—and several flowerbeds, again geometrically shaped, and these were backed by a breathtaking view of the bay, the distant headlands, and the open sea beyond. To the right of the lawn was a very large swimming-pool, cloverleaf-shaped, equipped with a double diving board and a chute, and a complex of changing-rooms and barbecue area. Partially visible beyond the complex was a helicopter pad.

Bennett, who was wearing swimming trunks, stood. In his late thirties or early forties, he had a strongly featured face, noticeable for a very square chin. He smiled freely, but it was a tight and not a warm smile and it was easy to guess that he reacted calculatingly rather than emotionally to any situation. His body was well muscled, showing none of the usual extra inches which came from luxurious living and his flesh was tanned a deep brown. He greeted them politely enough, but made no attempt to shake hands. With one quick glance, he identified Alvarez. 'You are the policeman?'

'Yes, señor. And my companion is Señor Ware, from England.'

'Well, I suggest we move into the shade before you tell me why you're here.' His tone was brisk and commanding —a man used to giving orders. He walked round to the open part of the pool complex where several comfortable chairs were set around a couple of glass-topped tables. 'I imagine you'd like something to drink?'

Ware asked for a gin and tonic and Alvarez, a brandy. Bennett opened up the top flaps of a mobile cocktail cabinet and this raised a shelf in which were bottles, glasses, and an insulated container. He unscrewed the lid of the container and looked inside, went over to the wall and used an intercom to ask for ice. This was brought by the woman who'd opened the front door. Bennett put two cubes of ice into each glass and the rest of them into the container. He carried the drinks to the table on a silver salver, and sat.

'What brings you here?'

Alvarez answered. 'I believe you knew Señor Timothy Green?'

'I don't think so.'

'He worked for you for several years,' said Ware.

Bennett looked at him. 'The Inspector introduced you, but did not explain the reason for your visit. Are you connected with the British police?'

'I'm a loss adjuster, acting for the Crown and Life Insurance Company.'

'Really? To the best of my knowledge, I've never had any dealings with that company.'

'Timothy Green took out a life insurance with them.'

'Should there be any significance in the fact as far as I'm concerned?'

'Señor,' said Alvarez, 'did you know that a week ago a light aeroplane, a Flèche, took off from the old airport on this island and crashed into the sea roughly half an hour later?'

'No, I didn't.'

'You don't read the local paper or watch television?'

'I read *The Times* and watch the BBC on satellite; there was no mention of the crash in either.'

'The aeroplane was piloted by Timothy Green, the man who worked for you in England.'

'I've remembered now that I did employ someone called Green—I don't know what his Christian name was—so it might just conceivably be the same person.'

'Did he visit you on the Thursday, Friday, or Saturday?'

'Had he done, I would have remembered him the moment you mentioned his name.'

'But he didn't?'

'I thought I'd just made that clear.'

'Do you own a boat, señor?'

'Yes. Why should the question concern you?'

'What kind is it?'

'A sixty-foot motor-cruiser.'

'Did you go out in it a week ago yesterday?'

'I really can't answer. I don't remember every time I take her out.'

'But surely you would remember if you went out that Saturday night to meet Señor Green?'

'I must have misunderstood you. I thought you said that Green was piloting a plane which crashed at sea?'

'That's right.'

'Then I could hardly have sailed out to meet him. Absurd things happen on this island, but hardly that absurd.'

'Not so absurd if you picked him up after he parachuted from the plane.'

'Far, far too absurd,' he said drily.

'Green was one of your salesmen,' said Ware.

'If he's the same man, that's correct.'

'He's been described as a man with a golden tongue. Was it his golden tongue, suitably barbed, which inveigled you into helping him fake his own death?'

Bennett said coldly: 'I've been very patient, but I do have

my limits and you've just breached them. Perhaps you'd be kind enough to leave.'

Alvarez looked across at Ware, then stood. 'We may wish to ask you further questions at another time.'

'Then I hope that you'll at least do me the credit of making them more intelligent.' He did not stand as they left.

The woman was waiting in the sitting-room. Ware said, his tone ironic: 'What's the betting he called her up on the intercom and told her to make certain that we don't pinch anything on our way out?'

They drove down the winding road to the gates, which opened as they came in sight of them. Once through the gateway and on the road, Ware said: 'What do you make of him?'

Alvarez answered carefully: 'He certainly acts like a great hidalgo.'

'If that means a cold, condescending bastard, I'll agree!'

'But perhaps his manner was telling us more than that he considers himself to be a great man. Someone who is afraid often attacks as a form of defence.'

'All right, let's assume he didn't like our questions one little bit. Where do we go from here?'

'To whichever restaurant we decide on. It's lunch-time.'

Ware laughed. 'You're a great man for getting your priorities right.'

It was after 4.30 when they walked along the eastern arm of the harbour to the harbourmaster's office, two rooms which were filled to overflowing with tables, bookcases, filing-cabinets, and instruments, and kept cool by air-conditioning and outside awnings.

The elderly harbourmaster shook his head. 'I know Señor Bennett's boat right enough since it's one of the largest in the harbour. But I've no idea whether she was at sea a week ago last night.'

'You don't keep a log of movements?'

'Normally, no; there's no reason to do so. It's very different if we've reason to suspect smuggling. Then we keep a close watch.'

'Of course.'

The harbourmaster was uncertain whether or not that had been said ironically.

'Which is his boat?'

'The last but one tied up at this quay. I don't remember her name, but she's a trawler yacht, with plenty of accommodation.'

'Have you ever been aboard it?'

'He's never asked me aboard. He's not a friendly man; polite, but not friendly.'

Alvarez translated what had been said. Ware asked: 'What do we do now?'

'We'll search the boat.'

'Without a search warrant?'

'Sometimes, things are easier in this country than they are in yours.' Alvarez thanked the harbourmaster and then they left the building and walked up the quay to the penultimate boat.

She was stern-fast to the quayside and a small gangway, with stainless steel stanchions and whitened ropes, was pushed inboard so that there was no immediate way of boarding. She was not beautiful, as was the powerful, narrow-hulled speedboat in the next berth, but there was no mistaking the fact that in heavy seas she would be a good boat to be aboard.

'You can reach further than I can,' said Alvarez, as he stared across at the stern. 'D'you think you can get hold of the gangway?'

'Not without risking a ducking in water that looks unhealthily filthy,' replied Ware. 'There's an English yacht four back and I saw a bloke varnishing the coaming. I'll ask if he'll lend us a boathook.'

He was gone less than a minute and he brought back a boathook whose wooden haft was stained and scarred. Using this, he drew the gangway aft until he could catch hold of the end and lower it to the quay. 'I'll run this hook back now because we can return the gangway without it.'

As Ware left, Alvarez began to climb the gangway. Absurdly, it was an ordeal severe enough to make him sweat since he suffered badly from altophobia and it was with an audible expression of relief that he stepped aboard. There was open deck, then an area enclosed by three bulkheads and deckhead that was, in effect, a fair-weather smoke-room. For'd of this was a door which proved to be locked. As Ware boarded, Alvarez took from his pocket a set of skeleton keys which he'd confiscated from a housebreaker several years before. The third one, after some skilful probing, worked the tumblers.

'You're a man of many talents!' said Ware.

He smiled briefly. 'Some of which I try to keep hidden.'

The 'midships and aft accommodation consisted of a master stateroom with bathroom, four other cabins and one bathroom, a saloon—with bar aft—and a galley; for'd were two small cabins and one shower-stall and head, obviously intended for the crew; up top was a very well equipped chartroom and for'd of this a small wheelhouse.

In the chartroom, Alvarez searched the drawers under the chart table and in the third one down found a log book. He read through the last few entries and whistled with quiet satisfaction. He carried the log through to the wheelhouse, where Ware was searching through a flag locker in which were kept national flags and those of the international code.

'From the look on your face, you've found something,' said Ware, as he straightened up after replacing the black and white 'third substitute' flag in its locker.

'Bennett's a very meticulous man who's obviously never realized that there are times when it pays to be slipshod. He keeps a detailed log of all his voyages and on the thirteenth he set sail from here at sixteen-thirty hours, arriving at Stivas on Sunday evening at twenty-two hundred; he sailed back from Stivas on Tuesday morning.'

'Where is that?'

'South of Barcelona. It used to be a small fishing port and their sardines, grilled over an open wood fire, were like . . .' He found it too difficult to do justice to their excellence. 'Now, it's one of the largest yacht harbours on the coast. And I haven't tasted a Stivas sardine in years.'

Ware leaned against the flag locker and stared out through one of the for'd ports. 'He sailed to the prearranged spot and showed special lights for identification. Green jumped and with his parachuting skill landed alongside. Once aboard, they continued on to Stivas . . . When they docked, they wouldn't have had to clear customs or immigration, would they?'

'No. But, of course, the boat might have been boarded by someone to make certain it had sailed from this island, as claimed.'

'Failing that, how do we prove that Green was aboard? How are we going to trace him ashore?'

'There are always people around; boat owners, boat bums, sightseers, port officials. But let's suppose he was lucky and no one observed him land or we can't find someone who did. If you'd been Green, what would you have done on arrival, remembering it's late at night? Would you have stayed aboard until the morning when everything's moving once more or would you have gone ashore immediately?'

'Immediately,' Ware answered. 'All the time I'm aboard, I'm at risk. As soon as I'm ashore, I can adopt a new identity.'

'Which we have to uncover.'

'That's the hard part, isn't it . . . Enrique, I've obviously got to go to Stivas, but I'm not going to get very far on my own. Imagine my stumbling through my dozen words of Spanish, asking around after a man whose name I don't know! Is there any chance you could come along with me?'

CHAPTER 6

Salas was his normal ungracious self. 'Yes. What is it?'

'I'm ringing in connection with the Green case, señor,' replied Alvarez.

'What about it?'

'A problem has arisen.'

'With you, problems are forever arising.'

'As you know, señor, inquiries show that the plane crashed into the sea and there can't be any doubts on that score.'

'A man with your talent for confusion can always produce doubts.'

'The question is, was Green in the plane when it crashed?'

Salas said, in tones of disbelief: 'Didn't you assure me beyond the slightest possibility of contradiction that he had died in the plane?'

'As a matter of fact . . .'

'And now you're trying to tell me that he may, after all, still be alive?'

'You did say, señor, that if I was certain he was dead, probably he was alive.'

It had been a mistake to believe Salas might find some wry amusement from the memory. 'When I said that, Inspector, I was indulging in an ironic flight of imagination. I should have known better than to believe that however wild the flight, it could ever hope to keep pace with you.'

'At the time I was not aware of the fact that—'

'I have to confess that I cannot begin to understand why fate has been so unkind to me. Had I ever done a whit less than my duty, had I even once been guilty of the slightest degree of incompetence, I could console myself with the thought that you were under my command because as a man sows, so must he be made to reap. But I am denied any such consolation.'

Alvarez waited, but when Salas said nothing more, he finally broke the silence. 'Señor Ware and I believe that Green parachuted from the plane to board a boat which landed him in Stivas. So inquiries need to be made there. Señor Ware has asked if I could go with him to make such inquiries because he will find it extremely difficult to make them on his own. All my expenses will be met by the company for whom he is working.'

'He is suggesting you accompany him?'

'Yes, señor.'

'Then the man's a fool.'

It had taken only nine years to transform Stivas from a small, timelessly peaceful fishing village into a tourist centre where time was expensive and peace was virtually unknown. The marina had been enlarged three times and was now filled with yachts, motor-cruisers, and power boats, very few of which flew the Spanish flag. Tax evasion was one industry that was not subject to cyclical fluctuations.

The harbourmaster's office was in a large building set at the west end of what had been the original harbour. The harbourmaster was a paunchy man who had grown so rich through his job that he was having great trouble in concealing his wealth. When he shook his head, his jowls wobbled. 'No, there's no way,' he said in Catalan.

'The motor-cruiser's a pretty big one, so someone may have remarked it.' Alvarez spoke in Mallorquin and they understood each other, although there were some differences between their vocabularies and pronunciations.

'You call her big? Here, we don't call a cruiser big until she's over thirty metres long and then it's a job to remember one from the other.'

Alvarez tried to look impressed. 'Still, I'd be very grateful if you'd ask all your chaps if any of them remembers the *Morag* coming into harbour.'

A moment later he led the way outside where the sharp sunshine unkindly highlighted the lines in his face, making him look both older than he was and sadder. 'I'm afraid he's not going to be much help,' he said.

'I gathered that,' replied Ware, 'without understanding a word.'

'We'll have to find out what we can for ourselves.'

They questioned boat owners, a couple of men who were revarnishing a large schooner, workers in a boatyard, and a diving team who were setting the piles for an extension to one of the jetties, and the answers were always the same: none of them could remember the *Morag* coming into harbour.

They had lunch at one of the restaurants which overlooked the harbour; the prices astounded Alvarez, even though he was used to those which were charged in the tourist areas of the island. Afterwards, they spoke to three elderly fishermen who were mending nets (a few berths had, much to the harbourmaster's annoyance, been reserved for them), but they could not help; neither, having questioned his staff, could the harbourmaster, as he quickly informed them when they returned to his office.

Alvarez mopped his face and neck with a handkerchief. 'All that we're left with now is our belief that he'd have gone ashore immediately and, since it was so late, booked in at a hotel.'

'Remembering that it has to be odds on that he assumed a different identity the moment he was ashore.'

'You don't have to remind me how difficult it's going to be!' said Alvarez lugubriously. Then he cheered up. 'Let's discuss the problem over a drink.'

The evening sun was still hot and they were glad of the shade of the overhead awning as they sat outside one of the dockside cafés. Alvarez drank, sighed with pleasure, put the glass down on the table. 'Foreigners booking into a hotel have to show their passports and fill in a card, so there's no problem to finding out the names of everyone who booked into a hotel that night. But would he have stayed in Stivas and how do we identify him under a new identity? . . . There's not another town of any size for roughly twelve kilometres and there'd have been no public transport so the only way he could have travelled out would have been by taxi. Wouldn't he have decided that a taxi-driver would be curious about a foreigner who at so late an hour went from here, where foreigners are specially catered for, to somewhere where perhaps they are not?'

'That sounds logical.'

'Then we will ask the municipal police to check all hotels and hostals and to draw up a list of men who booked in after the time of arrival, discarding any who were obviously on a package tour. Once we have the list, we'll send the numbers of their passports to London and ask if any is false.'

Following the previous request from Alvarez, a copy of Timothy Green's passport photograph was sent by air from London to Barcelona, where a special messenger collected it and took it down by train to Stivas. The coloured photograph was no better and no worse than average; Green had a forgettable face set under blond hair, the only immediate noticeable feature of which was a generous moustache.

A Telex message from London, concerning the passport numbers, arrived six hours later. One of the numbers was of a passport stolen, along with ten others, from a consulate in Greece. Alvarez checked that number against the list he held; Thomas Grieves had booked in at the Hotel Grande at 11.15 on the Sunday night.

'Eureka! . . . Isn't it extraordinary how often they stick to the same initials?' said Ware, speaking with considerable satisfaction. 'Legend has it that that's so that they can continue to use their silver-backed monogrammed hair-brushes, but who uses them in this day and age?'

A taxi took them along the front and then, beyond the marina, up the gently sloping land on the west side of the bay to the Hotel Grande.

It was clear that the hotel was grand in name only. There was litter on the floor of the lobby, plants in the unpolished brass containers were dusty, and the very small concessionary shop beyond the desk had in its display window only the kind of mementoes that a holidaymaker bought when his judgement had been badly affected by too much wine and sun.

The clerk behind the desk was tired and lethargic and it seemed to cost him considerable mental effort to decide to call the assistant manager. The latter, much more wide awake, asked Alvarez and Ware into his office. He cleared some files off a chair and then placed that, and another, in front of the desk. As he sat, he said: 'Now, Inspector, how can I help? I hope that there's nothing wrong as far as the hotel's concerned?'

'We're here because we're interested in a guest who stayed just over a week ago.'

'Is this connected with the inquiries the municipal police were making earlier on?'

'That's right.'

'They wanted the names of male guests who booked in after ten on Sunday night, the fourteenth; we had one.'

'And his name was Thomas Grieves. How long was he here?'

'Just the one night.'

'Can you say how he paid the bill on Monday morning —in cash, by credit card, or however?'

'Give me a moment and I'll be able to tell you.' The assistant manager swivelled his chair round, switched on a desktop computer, tapped out a series of numbers, read what appeared on the screen of the VDU, stood and went over to a small plastic case from which he brought out a floppy disk which he fed into the machine. He tapped out more numbers, then waited. 'This time last year I'd have opened a ledger and given you the answer within twenty seconds; now we're computerized and it takes five minutes to look up anything. That's called modernization!'

They dutifully laughed.

Line after line of writing appeared on the VDU and the assistant manager read down them. 'The account was for four thousand two hundred and fifty pesetas, including IVA; he paid in cash.'

'Did you see him at any time?'

'No. I go off duty at seven in the evening and don't come in at all on a Monday, which is my day off, unless there are problems.'

'Could you find out who did see him so that we can have a word?'

'The staff who were on duty then almost certainly won't be in the hotel right now, but I'll do what I can.'

During the next hour they spoke to a night doorman and desk-clerk, both resentful at being called back to the hotel while off duty. The doorman half remembered a guest who'd arrived late that Sunday night with very little luggage, but freely admitted that he couldn't begin to describe the man. The desk-clerk was considerably younger and cocky.

'Sure, I remember him,' he said, as he stood by the side of the assistant manager's desk. He wore a T-shirt, over a pair of shorts, which bore a message in English that would have made any maiden aunt blush violently.

'Did he speak Spanish?'

'Do the foreigners ever?'

'Then you speak English?'

'I speak it bloody good,' he replied proudly in English.

'D'you think you'd know him again?'

'Sure.'

'Then will you describe him?'

He started confidently, very quickly realized how unimpressive he sounded. 'He was tall and . . . He was pleasant enough. I mean, he wasn't looking down the side of his nose, like some of'em do . . .'

'How old was he?'

'Older than me, but nowhere near as old as you.'

This description confirmed Alvarez's previous assessment of the qualities of the young man. 'What shape was his face—round, oval, or square?'

'Well, it was . . . Kind of neither one nor the other . . . I mean, I didn't take all that close notice since I wasn't to know you'd be asking all these questions, was I?'

'Clean-shaven?'

'I'm . . . I'm not quite certain about that.'

'Perhaps it'll be quicker if you tell me exactly what you do remember about him?'

'His hair was light and kind of blond; like the Norwegian bints have.' He leered at them, suggesting torrid experiences with an endless succession of beautiful Norwegian girls. 'And you were talking about him being clean shaven. He had a moustache; I can remember that now.'

Alvarez took the photograph of Green from his pocket and handed it across. The clerk studied it. 'That's him, right enough.'

'You are sure of that?'

'Couldn't be surer.'

Alvarez took the photograph back. 'Right, that's all. Thanks.' The clerk left the office. Alvarez said to Ware: 'Did you manage to gather anything of what he said?'

'Only that he seemed to recognize Green from the photo.'

'He claims he does, but I don't trust the identification.' He turned and spoke in Mallorquin to the assistant manager. 'If I asked you how far I could accept that young man's judgement, what would you answer?'

'That he's always out to impress how clever and sharp he is.'

'Fair enough . . . There's one last thing. After the Englishman left on Monday, the bedroom will have been cleaned. There's always the off-chance he left something behind, so would you find out who did the work and arrange for us to have a word with whoever it was?'

'A lot of the girls come in from the surrounding villages and I can't speak to them until tomorrow morning because they'll have gone home by now.'

'We'll come back tomorrow, then. And please impress on the girls that we're interested in everything, even the contents of the wastepaper basket.'

CHAPTER 7

When they returned to the hotel the next morning, it was to find that the assistant manager had become a flustered man. 'I didn't know yesterday or naturally I'd have told you. Why didn't the silly girl say at the time?' He began nervously to knead his fingers together. 'It's extraordinary how stupid they can be. I mean, I wouldn't have eaten her! It wasn't her fault if the notice had fallen to the floor. Please understand, if I'd known about it, I'd have told you.'

Alvarez, who sat on the right-hand chair in front of the desk, smiled. 'I'd understand if I had the slightest idea what you're talking about!'

The assistant manager began to calm down. 'I spoke to the girls who are brought in by Minibus and discovered it was Alejandra who cleaned out Room 18. I told her to come to the office. Then when I started asking her whether she remembered the Englishman, she burst into tears. For ages I couldn't get any sense at all out of her; she seemed almost hysterical.'

'And when you did learn what was the trouble?'

'It seems the Englishman had put a "Do not disturb"

notice on his door, but the string had broken and it had fallen. She didn't notice it, knocked on the door, and when there wasn't an answer used her key to go in. She found that the Englishman was still there, with a woman.'

'They were screwing?'

'She won't say what was going on.'

'But I have to know.'

'She won't say because she's so scared I'll blame her for not seeing the notice.'

'You don't think it may be a little more complicated than that? You told me she's from one of the villages and I expect life there is very much the same as it is in an inland village on the island. Where there are tourists, anything goes; where there aren't, things are very different. On the beaches the girls go topless, in the inland villages they're not allowed to watch a television programme that may be a little too suggestive. I'd say she was so shocked and embarrassed by what she saw that she feels she became part of the corruption if she admits to seeing it.'

'I suppose that's possible,' said the assistant manager doubtfully, wondering if a young woman could still be so naïve even if she did come from a small and semi-isolated village.

Alvarez was silent for a moment, then he said: 'I think it'll be best if I talk to her on her own; you don't mind, do you?'

'Of course not.'

'That's kind of you. Then if you'll ask her to come here in about five minutes?'

The assistant manager left. Alvarez explained what was happening to Ware. 'If I'm right, my best chance of getting her to talk is if there's just her and me.'

'In other words, you want me out of the way?'

'I hope the suggestion doesn't offend you?'

'Doesn't begin to, more especially since I wouldn't understand a word . . . I'll clear off and find a coffee somewhere.'

'Remember that it's an old Mallorquin custom to add brandy to the morning coffee.'

'I'm a convinced traditionalist.' He left.

A few minutes later a young woman, neatly dressed, plain face made plainer by nervousness, sidled into the office.

'Hullo, Alejandra, come over here and sit down . . . My name's Enrique Alvarez and I'm from Mallorca. I understand you live in a nearby village?'

'Esteria,' she murmured as she sat on the edge of the chair.

'And how far from here is that?'

'About six kilometres.'

'It's rich countryside, isn't it? Much richer than where I come from; we've no green at this time of the year except where there's irrigation. Tell me, what kind of crops are mainly grown around Esteria?'

She had expected to be questioned sharply, perhaps even with some contempt, and initially she was constrained by surprise, then she relaxed and talked freely. Even when he finally introduced the subject of the Englishman in Room 18, she did not immediately revert back to her previous state of embarrassed nervousness.

'I didn't see the notice. But I did knock and there wasn't any sort of an answer. I promise you, there wasn't.'

'I don't doubt you for one second. So when you heard nothing, and because it was getting on in the morning, you naturally assumed he'd left and booked out; you unlocked the door and went in. What did you see?'

She looked down at the floor and shook her head.

'Just tell me slowly and remember, I know that it wasn't your fault and you'd have done anything rather than see what you did.'

'I . . . I can't.'

'I have to know, Alejandra. If you tell me now it'll be over and done with and probably there'll be no need ever again to mention it to anyone.'

She looked up at him, then away. After a while, she spoke in disjointed sentences, fiddling furiously with one of the buttons of her apron as she did so. She had stepped into the room and been so shocked that initially she'd been unable to understand the details of what she was looking at. Then these had become all too clear. The man, naked, had been lying on the bed. The woman, wearing black garter-belt, fish-net stockings, and leather boots, had been whipping him.

'Could you see his face?'

'When he realized I was there, he turned towards me and shouted something.'

'What?'

'I don't know. It was in English. But . . . but it sounded terrible.'

'Can you describe him?'

She couldn't. The general scene was brutally etched into her memory, but her confusion and embarrassment had been so great that she could recall nothing specific about the two participants.

There was, he judged, nothing more to be learned from her. He tried to explain that she had absolutely no cause to feel the slightest sense of shame because she had inadvertently witnessed such a scene, but wasn't certain that his words had much effect. He wished her father good crops and then opened the door for her. She was about to pass through the doorway when she stopped. 'I've forgotten to tell you something. I . . . I just couldn't go back to do the room after they'd gone, so Carmina cleared it out. She found a book.'

'What kind of a one?'

'A paperback; guests often leave them behind.'

'Would you know what happened to it?'

'It was in English, so she won't have kept it. She probably sold it to the bookshop because we're allowed to do that with books that are left.'

'Is Carmina in the hotel now?'

'She's doing the rooms.'

'Then would you be kind enough to ask her to come and have a word with me?'

Carmina was unlike Alejandra. Self-confident, pert, she wore considerable make-up and the dress under the maid's apron was tight across her breasts and short in hem.

Alvarez introduced himself, then said: 'I think you cleaned Room 18 a week ago on Monday?'

'Suppose I did?'

'You found that a paperback had been left behind. I'd like to know what you did with it?'

'Sold it, along with some others, like we're allowed to.'

'You sold it to whom?'

'The shop along the front what buys foreign books.'

'When was this?'

She shrugged her shoulders. 'End of last week, when I'd enough to make it worthwhile. The old buzzard who runs the place won't buy just one or two.'

'Can you remember the title of the book?'

She giggled. 'No, but the cover was hot stuff.'

'In what way?'

'What way d'you think?'

'I don't, because there are too many ways to choose from.'

The answer seemed to annoy her, perhaps because it was clear he found her boring rather than amusingly salacious. She said bad-temperedly: 'It showed a naked woman whipping a man.'

'Was he naked as well?'

'Interested?'

'Yes, but not for the reason you think.'

'He wasn't wearing anything, but part of him was hidden.' She giggled again as she looked quickly at him. 'Had to be, didn't it?'

He said he'd asked her all the questions he wanted to and then followed her out of the office, branching off to cross the lobby to the main entrance. There, he spoke to the doorman to find out whether he'd seen a man bring a woman into the hotel on the Monday morning.

'There's men and women coming in here all the time.'

'I'm talking about a woman who like as not was a prostitute.'

'How would I know what she is?'

'You'd know.'

'Well, I didn't.'

'You are quite sure of that?'

'Look,' said the doorman aggressively, 'I do my job and I don't set out to make trouble.'

'Meaning that if you're tipped well you don't see a whore even when she's a metre in front of you?'

'There've been no whores in here. And anyway, if there's no fuss, who gets hurt?'

It was not a question he was prepared to answer. 'Suppose I asked you to identify her.'

'I've just said, there wasn't no one.'

Alvarez returned into the hotel and, after a quick word with the receptionist who told him where to go, walked round to the patio on the south side of the hotel where Ware was sitting at a table near the central fountain which wasn't working.

'Did you have any luck?' Ware asked.

'Up to a point. When Alejandra entered the bedroom, she was faced by a flagellation scene.'

'Was she indeed! Which one of 'em was wielding the whip?'

'The woman.'

'So he's a masochist. They say it takes all sorts to make the world; some of them just seem a bit more assorted than others. Can the girl identify Green?'

'She can't begin to identify either of them. She was so shocked, she hasn't any memory of what they looked like.'

'Damn!'

'I know. Had it been Carmina who'd surprised them, we'd have had exact descriptions.'

'Then where do we go from here?'

'We will make inquiries among the car hire firms and at the railway station to see if we can discover how he left and where he went.' A waiter was passing and Alvarez called him over and ordered a coffee solo and a brandy. 'But,' he continued, 'I don't think we can hope to learn much from either source. At this time of the year, the car-hire firms are so busy that they won't remember anyone unless they had cause to and he'll have tried to make certain there wasn't any; but there will be their records, so would he have hired a car which meant he needed a driving licence in his new name as well as the passport and there would be difficulties when it came to crossing borders? Much more likely he'll have gone by train. But is a booking clerk ever going to remember his buying a ticket, especially when we've no idea of his destination?'

Ware stared into the distance, frowning slightly, then he relaxed. 'Even if you're right to be so pessimistic, we can be ninety-nine per cent certain we now know what happened.'

'But my superior chief is only just content with one hundred per cent! . . . I have forgotten to mention that we may just have one more lead. When the bedroom was finally cleared by Carmina, she found an English paperback had been left behind. It's a recognized perk of chambermaids to collect up any books left behind and to sell them to a bookshop which specializes in foreign ones for the tourists. If we could trace it, there's the slight chance it might offer a lead—I'm thinking of a point-of-sale label, or something of that nature. Unfortunately, though, she can't remember the title of the book, only that the cover shows a naked woman whipping a man. There are, perhaps, not so many people who buy a book with such a cover?'

'Depends on how many ex-public schoolboys have stayed in Stivas recently.'

Twenty minutes later they took a taxi—Alvarez declined to walk—down to the front road. The bookshop offered escapist entertainment rather than intellectual stimulation; the thousands of paperbacks, on revolving stands, stacked up on tables, and filling endless shelves, were printed in English, French, German, Dutch, and Swedish.

Alvarez spoke to the owner, who sat at a counter on which were so many books that he was only visible through the small, and necessary, gap by the till. 'You buy books from the staff at the Hotel Grande?'

The owner, who had a long, thin, complaining face, spoke in antagonistic tones. 'I buy books from the staff of all the hotels.'

'Do you know Carmina?'

'I don't know the names of any of 'em.'

'She came in here at the end of last week and sold you several paperbacks.'

'So?'

'I'd like to know where those books are now?'

'With the rest of 'em, of course.'

'It'll save you a lot of trouble if you can remember whereabouts among all the others.'

The owner looked even more morose. 'You said they came in at the end of last week? Then like as not, I've not been through 'em yet.'

'What does that mean?'

'That they'll still be in the back room, waiting for sorting and pricing.'

'I'd like to see where.'

Reluctantly, the owner climbed down from the stool. He unlocked the counter flap, after moving a number of books off this and swearing as he did so, and Alvarez and Ware went through and into the room beyond which smelled of old dust. Everywhere there were books, mostly paperbacks, stacked in piles which in many cases had collapsed so that it seemed to be a scene of confusion, yet the owner unhesitatingly led the way over to two piles, still intact, that were near the dirt-stained, fly-speckled window. 'That's where they'll be; can't say which ones.' He left them.

Alvarez pointed to one pile. 'Will you take that one and I'll look through the other?'

Ware's had been the smaller pile and he was the first to finish. He straightened up. 'Naked and near-naked ladies by the score, but none of them enjoying herself with a whip.'

Alvarez had three more books to check. The second one had a cover which depicted a naked and very generously endowed lady who was about to strike a naked man who knelt beyond her, his honour carefully screened by her right leg. 'I think we've found it!' He examined the paperback. Its condition suggested it had been bought recently and only read once. There was no point-of-sale tag and no writing on any of the front or back pages. He held out the covers and shook and a slip of paper fell out and fluttered to the ground. He picked this up and saw that it was a receipt, issued by Campsa, at Palma airport, dated Saturday July 15 and timed at 2108 hours, for four hundred litres of fuel. He handed the receipt to Ware. 'I can now tell my superior chief that we are a hundred per cent certain.'

CHAPTER 8

When Ware's father had died, he'd left behind him as many debts as friends; he'd been a man who'd stand drinks all round in the clubhouse while in his pocket was a letter from his bank manager reminding him that his overdraft had risen above the agreed limit and would he please take immediate steps to reduce it. At the time of his death, Ware had been old enough to understand that the reason for the straitened circumstances in which the family suddenly found itself was his father's improvidence and this knowledge had

had a very great effect on him. By nature of the same happy-go-lucky, devil-take-tomorrow character, he would probably have lived a heedless life had he not been forced to appreciate that the cost of selfish happiness came high and it was a cost which often had to be met by others. Now, there were times when Heather, his wife, wondered how he could be two such different people. He would suggest in all seriousness an exotic and expensive holiday in some far-off place and yet on the same day worry at length because their electricity bill had risen slightly. Paradoxically, this contradiction helped him in his job. He had the imagination to visualize possibilities that would never occur to a sobersides, yet would conduct an investigation with a perseverance and attention to detail a more carefree investigator would scorn.

He and the claims manager of the Crown and Life Insurance Company sat on opposite sides of the long, well polished table in the conference room on the fourth floor of the Edwardian building in Eastley Street.

Parrot—to his annoyance, his nose was slightly beaked—tapped the four-page report in front of himself. 'You don't think that perhaps the evidence is somewhat stronger than you're suggesting?'

'That depends, of course, whether you're talking in terms of fact or law. I don't doubt that he faked his own death, was picked up in Bennett's boat, landed in Stivas, spent the night at the Hotel Grande, had a constitutional whipping in the morning, and then took off to parts unknown. But try to prove all that in a court of law and counsel would be very quick to point out how everything's virtual supposition.'

'Not the fuel receipt you found in the paperback.'

'We can't prove that the man in the hotel was Green, only that he was travelling on a false passport and probably had light or blond hair and a moustache; we can't prove that the paperback in the bookshop was left behind by him;

we can't prove that the receipt was used as a bookmarker by the same man who bought the fuel . . . A clever counsel would revel in all those negatives. As I see things, until we can prove beyond all legal doubt that Green survived the air crash, we cannot say that if taken to court we must win the case.'

'Even so, you don't reckon that our best bet is to wait for a claim to be made and then to refuse to pay it? After all, when the other side sees the strength of our case they might very well drop out because if we present the evidence we have this might very well attract the attention of the police, who'd carry out a much more thorough investigation than you ever can, which could easily uncover the missing proof.'

'I still think it's worth my digging a little deeper. If I could find his girlfriend, there's the chance I'd be able to get a lead on where he's hiding out and that would settle everything, once and for all.'

Parrot fiddled with a pencil. 'All right,' he said finally. 'See if you can track her down.'

In her early twenties, Joan Carling had been physically very attractive and so had had a large number of boyfriends. Unfortunately, she had accepted their homage as her due and such self-satisfaction had cooled their ardours even more quickly than her rapidly expressed distaste for 'mucking around'. Consequently, on her twenty-eighth birthday she had looked in a mirror and had seen a woman who was obviously beginning to age and all of whose contemporaries were married. She had panicked.

Born and brought up in Wimbledon, her tastes were refined, her manners impeccable, and her values irreproachable. She carried her shopping in a Harrods bag, was invariably polite to the lower orders, and voted Conservative. Despite all this, when Timothy Green—who clearly had not been even to a minor public school—suggested a dinner date, she had not refused him. And when, a few meetings later, he had begun to fondle her breasts, she had consoled herself with the thought that at least on her twenty-ninth birthday she would not still be unmarried.

Being so conscious of her background, after they were married she had not hesitated to show him in which areas he lacked breeding. That he was a salesman was a cause for apology, that he was a very successful one who made a great deal of money in no way mitigated the social solecism; that he made a noise when he drank soup from the end of the spoon instead of the side was of far more concern than that he was so generous-hearted that he did all he could to please her despite her attitude towards him.

After he had lost his job and his large income, there had been little reason to continue to suffer him since it was the state of marriage that was important in her circle, not the success, or otherwise, of it. She had demanded a separation. Her father—Harrow, Lloyds, a silent soup-drinker—had, despite many years of heavy drinking, gambling, and expensive mistresses, left her enough money to be reasonably financially secure, but naturally she had demanded the house and made certain she got it. Some time later, he'd asked if she'd agree to a divorce, only to learn that if he thought she was going to give her blessing to his luring another woman into his disgusting embraces . . .

His death irritated her because it raised a question to which she did not know the answer. What was the correct degree of mourning to observe in respect of a prurient, adulterous husband?

Ware arrived at her house at a quarter past eleven and she was reasonably welcoming since he spoke without a regional accent and was well, if a shade informally, dressed.

'I'll be as brief as I can,' he said. 'I represent the Crown and Life Insurance Company with whom your husband took out a fairly large life insurance roughly three years ago.'

'He did what?'

'Then you didn't know about it?'

She shook her head.

He hid his surprise; she had struck him as a woman who would have made certain she knew everything about her husband's affairs. 'As I'm sure you'll understand, in connection with that policy, certain facts have to be verified.' He spoke carefully because he did not want to have to be the person who told this sharp-eyed, straight-mouthed woman that her husband was, in fact, alive, living with a girlfriend, and probably not intending to share any of his fraudulently acquired insurance money with his estranged wife. At the conclusion he said: 'I imagine you have a copy of his will?'

'Naturally.'

'May I have a look at it?'

She left the room, to return with a long, brown envelope which she handed to him.

It was a short, simple will made immediately after the marriage. Everything Green owned was to go to his wife and, surprisingly, there was no proviso should she predecease him. Ware noted the name and address of the solicitor on the back of the envelope before returning it. He thanked her and left.

It took him twenty minutes to find the solicitor's offices, largely thanks to a misdirection which sent him down to the wrong end of the high street and thence into a maze of one-way streets. The rambling building was in need of decoration and the carpet in front of the information desk was nearly threadbare. This reminded him of some advice he'd once been given. 'If you want a smart lawyer in central London, go to one who has smart offices; in the suburbs or the country, to one whose offices need money spent on them.'

He met a partner who dressed and spoke as if he regularly rode to hounds.

'Let me see, Mr Ware, if I have the facts correctly. The

Spanish authorities are at the moment satisfied he died in the air crash and so are in the process—likely to be drawn out for normal administrative reasons—of issuing a death certificate. You, however, contend that he did not die in the crash?'

'That's right.'

'Your interest in the matter is clear. If he is alive, the company you represent will not be liable to pay out the sum assured on his life. You are unconcerned with the criminal aspect of the matter?'

'Unconcerned, if that means that I have no interest in whether or not he is ever prosecuted for attempted fraud.'

'I ask because the distinction does raise an interesting point. If he died in the crash, his valid will—in due course of time—becomes open to public inspection; in the circumstances, I might be able to find the justification for letting you read it now. If he is alive, his will is secret and there cannot be any justification for my divulging any of its details. Mrs Green has informed me of his death and I had begun to set in motion all the usual steps. Now, you tell me he may well be alive which brings all such steps to a stop . . . I think I must refuse your request, Mr Ware. Until the position is absolutely clear, my duty now must be to act as if he were alive.'

Ware said ruefully: 'I was afraid of that.'

The partner smiled briefly. 'Had you not made the strength of your belief so evident . . . I gain the impression that you assume he will have made a new will relatively recently?'

'He must have done. Mrs Green showed me one, made immediately after their marriage, in which she gets everything. He'll have cut her out in favour of his girlfriend. The insurance money must be paid to a named person whom he can trust not to run off with it and it's difficult to think of anyone else he'd be willing to trust in the face of such temptation.'

'You would appear to have rather a poor opinion of people's honesty.'

'I've been a loss adjuster for several years.'

'Quite! Assume you're correct, if you knew the name of the beneficiary, and his or her address, would you expect Mr Green to be living with such person now?'

'He's smart; very smart except when he becomes either too greedy or too pressed for time. So I very much doubt that he's living with her yet, just in case someone turns up to question her about him. He'll be keeping out of sight, but in contact, and that's how it'll be until the money's paid out. Assuming it ever is.'

'Then if you knew where his friend lives, you would no longer have a pressing interest in his valid will?'

'All I want is her name and address.'

'Information provided outside a will which although pertinent to that will is not specifically material to any of the terms in it, clearly comes under the umbrella of client confidentiality, but this may be less absolute than that pertaining to wills. In other words, if the provision of such information is to the advantage of the estate, it may be given. It is clearly to the advantage of Mr Green's affairs that I know whether or not he died in the air crash. I feel, therefore, that I shall be justified if I give you the name and address of the person to whom all matters of importance are to be referred in the event of his death.'

Lawyers, thought Ware, were surely the most successful of all practitioners of the art of subtle hypocrisy.

CHAPTER 9

Although Ware had always liked the French, he'd never managed to become reconciled to their determined inability to understand their own language when incorrectly spoken by a foreigner. He leaned his head through the open car window and for the third time asked directions to the Rue de la Paix, and for the third time the elderly man on the pavement shrugged his shoulders. 'Forget it,' Ware said in English. The Frenchman inclined his head—in contempt, in triumph, in commiseration?—and walked on.

Ware studied the small road map of Changres which the car-hire firm had given him at the airport and he tried to work out why, since he had taken the third road to the right after the cross-roads, he had turned into Rue Mortel which, to add to the confusion, wasn't marked. A woman, past her youth but maturely smart and very aware of that fact, approached. He leaned out through the window and asked her to help him and this time his accent was an advantage since it marked him as a foreigner and she had a soft spot for the underprivileged. She listened to his halting French and then replied in good English that he was in Rue de la Paix, but the name had recently been changed to Rue Mortel to commemorate the town's late mayor. He thanked her and she walked on, satisfied that although he was considerably younger than she, he would be watching her.

He left the car and walked along the pavement, past houses which had been built at the turn of the century for the well-to-do bourgeoisie and whose rather bleak exteriors gave no indication of the elegance to be found within many of them. He reached No. 45, pressed the entry button, and the door latch slipped free with a quick buzz. There was a short passage, to the right-hand side of which were the concierge's rooms, to the left-hand side stairs, and at the end a small courtyard.

He climbed the stairs to the third floor. There were two flats on each floor and in the small brass holder on the left-hand side of the landing was a handwritten card naming Miss S. Collins. He rang the bell.

The door was opened by a woman he judged to be in her early thirties. 'Miss Collins? My name is Robert Ware.' She was not beautiful, yet she had a face which attracted because it expressed character; by some visual trick, it seemed to alter in composition when seen from different angles. Her brown eyes were warm, but her nose had a touch of Roman arrogance; her mouth was generous and her lips full, suggesting a capacity for passion; her hair was black and wavy and cut tightly to the shape of her head; she wasn't fashionably thin, but neither was she plump. A woman to remember and to wonder about. 'May I have a word with you?'

'What about?'

There was a touch of huskiness in her voice which reminded him of a distant cousin who rode sidesaddle. He did not answer immediately, but brought out his wallet and from this extracted a card which he handed to her.

She read it, looked up. 'I don't understand.'

'I'd like to discuss something that concerns us both.'

'But what? I've never heard of this insurance company before. How can anything to do with it concern me?'

'A few years ago Mr Timothy Green took out a life insurance with them.'

'Oh! . . .' She turned away so that he could no longer see her face. 'I . . . I can't . . .' Her voice trailed off into silence.

'I'm very sorry, but I do have to talk to you,' he said firmly. It was, he thought, a tribute to her acting ability that until he reminded himself that it was ridiculous, he felt guilty because he was causing her such distress.

She did not move for several seconds, then, shoulders slumped, she stepped back. He accepted this as an invitation to enter, closed the door.

'I . . . I just can't get used to knowing he's dead,' she murmured.

He noticed, for the first time, the black armband she wore. Since Green must have considered a visit such as the present one to be unlikely, it was a tribute to his skilful planning that he had still taken the possibility into account and arranged for her to wear a sign of mourning. Skilful planning negated by greed or the necessity to be greedy.

She led the way into the sitting-room. Large, with a high ceiling, originally it would have been sombrely decorated and furnished to provide a fitting setting in which a grave and dignified paterfamilias could digest his lunch and dream of mistresses, but now it had been painted in an off-white, the furniture was modern and occasionally frivolous, and the four modern paintings on the walls were filled with colour if little form.

She sat in a rocking-chair and began to rock, staring out through the nearer window as she did so. He studied her face which was in profile. He saw strength and determination. Perhaps she had agreed to help in the proposed fraud without any of the hesitations and fears that most women would have experienced. Before, he had assumed that Green had been much the stronger of the team; now he was certain that if she had not wanted to help him, no amount of cajoling on his part would have persuaded her to do so. He said: 'Miss Collins, how did you hear about Mr Green's death?'

She rocked twice before she said sharply: 'What does that matter?'

'It could be important.'

'Oh God, can't you understand . . .?'

He waited, then said: 'Either I or the police have to question you. I promise you it will be easier if I do so.'

'Why d'you say that? Why should the police bother me?'

'If you'll answer the question I asked a moment ago, I'll tell you.'

She continued rocking for several seconds, then abruptly checked the movement with her feet. She ran the tip of her tongue over her full lips. 'He didn't return here when he said he would. I thought maybe business had taken longer than he'd expected, then I wondered if the weather had stopped him flying back, so I rang his hotel in Majorca. They told me . . .' She stopped.

'They said that his plane had crashed at sea.'

She closed her eyes, resumed rocking.

'His plane did crash at sea. But as you well know, he was not in it when it crashed.'

She spoke fiercely. 'What d'you mean?'

'He parachuted from the plane and was picked up by a boat which landed him on the mainland.'

'If that had happened, he'd have got in touch with me immediately. Why have you come here with such filthy lies? Oh God, isn't it enough to have to know he's dead, without having someone like you taunt me . . .'

'I'm not taunting you, Miss Collins.' His tone was sad, because he hated having to convince her that all their plans had failed. 'Green needed money and he decided to fake his own death so that a claim could be made against his life insurance. In his last will he named you as sole beneficiary, thereby making certain you'd be paid the insurance money. He hired a twin-engined Flèche and flew to Mallorca where he persuaded a past employer of his to cooperate in the fraud. He then flew from the island and rendezvoused with a motor-cruiser, jumped from the plane and parachuted down, and was picked up. The plane crashed several minutes later.

'The motor-cruiser sailed to Stivas and presumably he telephoned you on arrival to let you know that everything had gone according to plan. He stayed one night in the Hotel Grande before leaving Stivas. Exactly where he is now I don't know; you most certainly do.'

'That's all filthy lies.'

'We both know it's the truth.'

'He's dead. He never phoned me. D'you hear, he's dead.'

'Miss Collins, a Spanish detective and I went to Stivas and talked to the employees at the Hotel Grande, where he used the name Thomas Grieves. We also had his passport number checked and it turned out to belong to a passport which had been stolen.'

'That doesn't prove anything.'

'On the contrary, it proves that Grieves was not who he claimed to be.'

'Just because a man has a false passport . . .'

He interrupted, determined to make her understand that it was hopeless to go on arguing. 'A desk clerk made a reasonable identification of him from his passport photo. Next morning, a chambermaid went into the bedroom, not realizing he was still there, and he was on the bed . . .'

'Is she trying to say that that man was Tim?'

He shook his head. 'She's unable to identify him, but what's important . . .'

'That's important. She can't identify him because he wasn't Tim.'

'She can't identify him because . . .' He stopped.

'What?'

'The actual reason is immaterial.'

'No, it isn't. You come here making filthy accusations, saying Tim isn't dead and he's a crook, but you won't answer a simple question. It proves you're lying.'

'She couldn't identify him because she was so shocked by what she saw,' he said reluctantly. 'He wasn't alone. There was a woman with him; he was naked and she was wearing standard s/m gear and was whipping him.'

She gave a short cry, put her hand to her mouth.

'I'm very sorry,' he said sincerely.

She turned away, but not before he saw that now tears were flooding from her eyes. For the first time her grief was bitterly genuine because for the first time she had learned that he had perversely betrayed her. He spoke quickly. 'The chambermaid left and later another girl cleaned up the room once it was vacated. She found an English paperback had been left behind and she sold this, with some others, to a bookshop in Stivas. We identified the book and found in it a receipt for aviation fuel which had been issued at Palma airport. The airport records show that that receipt refers to the Flèche which Green was flying. So we can prove that Grieves, who stayed the night at the hotel, was really Green.'

There was a long silence, broken only by the sounds of the rocking-chair. Finally he asked, quietly, sympathetically: 'Will you tell me where he is now?'

'He's dead.'

Even now, knowing she had been betrayed, she was yet not prepared to betray. He knew a surge of admiration for her and it was because of this emotion that he said: 'If no claim is made against the policy, then as far as Crown and Life are concerned there will be no need to initiate any action. The English police have not yet been advised of the facts because until and unless a claim is made there is only evidence that Mr Green is alive, not that there's been an attempted fraud. Because the company is English, he is English, the plane was British registered, and the crash occurred in international waters, the Spanish police are not directly involved.' She was staring into the far distance. 'Do you understand what I am trying to tell you?'

She gave no answer, nor did she withdraw her gaze.

'Miss Collins, persuade him that it really is in both your interests not to make any claim under the insurance.'

'Go away.'

He left the flat. As he walked down the stairs, he wondered why life could be so bitterly unfair that a woman of her character fell in love with a man so perverted that it was a pleasure to have a woman whip him.

CHAPTER 10

The morning was exceptionally hot and the humidity was high so that the atmosphere in the office was oppressive even though the window was open and a fan working. Alvarez was slumped in his chair and contemplating infinity when the phone rang to jerk him fully awake. He looked at his watch. A quarter to one. Very soon he could stop work and return home for lunch. He lifted the receiver.

'Enrique? It's Robert here. I thought you'd want to know how things have gone. I managed to track down Serena Collins, Green's girlfriend, and I went over to Changres, in eastern France, to talk to her . . . But before I tell you what happened, just answer something, will you? What kind of woman do you imagine she is?'

He leaned back in the chair. 'I can only judge from the little we've learned about him. He's clever, prepared to take risks, and no respecter of the law; but he's also a deviant, which means a serious weakness of character and that in turn suggests he's a boaster, trying to hide such weakness . . . He'd want a woman who'd enhance his image, someone who draws other men's eyes and evokes their jealousy.'

'Exactly how I reasoned. And we couldn't be more wrong. She's not the least bit like that. She's not young and tarty, but mature, warm, and charming. So what's she doing with him?'

Alvarez was surprised on two accounts; that Serena Collins was such a woman as Ware had just descibed; that Ware should speak about her with such open, forceful admiration. 'Perhaps she doesn't, or won't, understand the kind of man he really is. Obviously, she knows about the intended insurance fraud since she has to be part of it, but, as we've said before, a lot of people don't regard the defrauding of an insurance company as a serious crime. Which leaves his perversion. Perhaps he's managed to keep this hidden from her.'

'I'd have thought that someone of her nature would instinctively realize that there was something rotten about him.'

'If so, then she condones his behaviour or even indulges his desires.'

'That's a disgusting suggestion. Quite impossible.'

It was, thought Alvarez, difficult to understand the sharpness of Ware's reactions to the suggestion except on the grounds of jealousy. Yet there had never been the slightest suggestion other than that Ware was a very happily married man so how could he become jealous after so brief an acquaintance? Alvarez shrugged his shoulders. Experience proved again and again that when it came to the nature of the relationship between a man and a woman there were no reliable precedents, guide lines, or rules. He changed the course of the conversation. 'How did she react to your questioning?'

'She's a good actress and very determined and never once gave an inch, not even when I explained how strong was our proof. Nothing will make her admit that Green is alive.'

'So what did you do?'

'There wasn't anything I could do except try to make her understand that if no claim is made on the company, there's a chance Green—and she—will escape prosecution since I imagine it would be difficult to prove he deliberately crashed the plane unless Bennett gave the game away and admitted it was all prearranged.'

'Do you think that when she tells him, he'll accept the advice?'

'She's smart and determined and more than capable of making him forget his greed and see sense. I'll give you two to one that there's no claim.'

'Then from your point of view, the visit was successful.'

'Yes. But I . . .' He stopped.

Alvarez wondered what was the unspoken qualification?

They talked generalities for a short while, then Ware said goodbye and rang off. Alvarez stared with dislike at the mass of papers on his desk, mentally threw them aside, yawned, checked the time and regretfully decided he'd better wait another five minutes before leaving the post. He settled back in the chair and thought again about the odd way in which Ware appeared to be behaving. Of course, he shouldn't forget that Ware was still relatively young and inexperienced and therefore liable to make a fool of himself over women. A man had to be fully mature before he learned sexual wisdom. He found the thought a comforting one since it was not always easy to reconcile oneself to maturity.

As Alvarez finished pouring out two generous brandies for Jaime and himself, they heard a call from the front room. Jaime shouted at the kitchen: 'There's someone here.'

Dolores appeared in the doorway. 'Who is it?'

'How would I know?'

'By getting on your feet and finding out. Or have you already drunk far too much to go anywhere on your own two feet?'

'I haven't touched a drop yet,' he protested, indicating the brandy and forgetting all the wine previously consumed. 'In any case, it's woman's work to greet a visitor.'

She stepped into the room, took off her apron and dropped it over the back of a chair, and then, as she walked towards the far doorway, said scornfully: 'With you, everything but drinking is woman's work.'

Jaime waited until she'd gone through to the front room before he said: 'But she's a wonderful cook.' It was his way of excusing himself for having remained silent in the face of her provocative words.

They drank.

Dolores called out: 'Enrique, come here.'

He emptied his glass, pushed it across the table so that Jaime could refill it in his absence, stood, and walked through to the front room. Dolores was talking to an elderly woman, dressed in black, the colour and texture of whose face spoke of endless summers in the fields.

'It's Elena,' snapped Dolores, mortified that Alvarez obviously did not immediately identify their visitor.

'But of course!' He went forward and kissed her on both

cheeks, having to bend down to do so because, although short himself, the top of her head only came level with his chin. It was, he considered, small wonder that he had failed to recognize her. In the four years since the death of her only son, she had aged ten.

She looked up at him, her expression entreating. 'You will find them, won't you? They haven't been home for three days now.'

'Who are you talking about?'

'Miguel and Carlos.'

'Are you saying they've been missing since Sunday, but no one knows about it?'

She nodded.

'Why on earth haven't you reported their disappearance?'

Elena stared down at the tiled floor.

'Were they, then, on a trip?'

She nodded.

'How long did they expect to be away from home?'

'Just the one night. But they haven't come back. I thought there must be a delay and they'd stayed to wait for another night, but they've never turned up and I haven't heard a word. Where can they be? I said to Ana . . . She married Miguel and God has given them one fine boy and now she carries another in her belly. Carlos is not married yet, although he has a novia.'

'It's good to hear about Miguel . . . Tell me, what did you say to Ana?'

'That we must ask someone to help. She reminded me about you. You will help us, won't you, because we are relatives?'

Elena was only a very distant cousin of Dolores and the relationship between himself and Dolores was almost as remote, so that it was quite beyond him to work out the degree of relationship between Elena and himself, but for a Mallorquin even the most tenuous of relationships created an obligation. 'Of course I'll do everything I can.'

'There mustn't be any trouble,' she said nervously.

'He'll make certain there'll be none,' said Dolores.

'But although I'll naturally try and avoid . . .' he began.

'There'll be none.'

He gloomily wondered if Dolores had the slightest idea how difficult it might be to conceal his inquiries.

Dolores turned to Elena and suggested she stayed for a drink—if the men had left anything—but Elena said no, she had to return home to help Ana with the baby.

'Enrique will drive you back.'

The finca was along a dirt track, rough enough to rattle continuously the suspension of Alvarez's car. Except for the installation of electricity and running water, the house had not been reformed and there was still no glass in the upstairs windows which were protected by solid wooden shutters. Yet that this lack of modernization was not due to lack of money was made obvious by the new Renault 25 parked to the side of the house. In the field which surrounded the house were rows of beans, peppers, melons, lettuces, aubergines, and tomatoes, growing around orange, lemon, fig, and pomegranate trees; there were also a few roses, zinnias and geraniums in a small square, despite the fact that this land was good enough to grow more vegetables.

'You've some fine crops,' he said, as he climbed out of the car and studied the land.

For the first time, a little of the worry left her face.

'I've not seen better this year.'

'And you won't!'

From within came the cry of a baby and she hurried inside. Alvarez followed her. The first room had been furnished without regard to cost—the three-piece suite was in white leather, the large sideboard was heavily carved in a traditional Andalucian pattern, the clock above the open fireplace was of Swiss make and in an elaborate gilt frame, the colour TV had a twenty-five inch screen and the video was the very latest, capable of endless tricks with windows. Yet the floor was uneven and many of the ancient and stained tiles were cracked and needed replacing.

Ana was rocking a baby in her arms. She was attractive in a young, full-flowering way, but already her features were beginning noticeably to coarsen and it was easy to judge that in another five years she would have lost most of her looks.

'What's the matter with Pedro?' fussed Elena.

'Just wind.'

'Let me have him. I know how to get rid of it.'

'He's all right with me,' she said resentfully, holding the child more tightly to herself.

Different generations, thought Alvarez, were finding it ever harder amicably to live together; forty years before, Ana would have handed over the baby without a moment's hesitation, satisfied that an older generation must know more than she did.

Elena was annoyed, but did not pursue the matter. 'Enrique has said he'll find out what's happened to Miguel and Carlos.'

Ana nodded; she'd never doubt that he would.

Alvarez sat in one of the armchairs. 'How much do you know about the trip they were going on?'

The two women looked at each other; Elena answered. 'Only that they didn't expect to be away more than the one night.'

'You've no idea what they were collecting, where, or who they were to deliver to?'

'Of course not.'

'At what time did they sail on Sunday?'

It was Ana who answered. 'They left here at the end of the afternoon.'

'Have they been working with anyone else recently?'

'With no one.'

He wondered if they'd really told him all they knew or if, out of a misguided sense of security, they were keeping some facts from him.

CHAPTER 11

In just a few years, the islanders had experienced dramatic changes in their lives, yet in the main they had not let such changes blind them to the fact that man kept his identity by holding to certain truths: God and the family were to be honoured (yet many Mallorquin everyday expressions were shockingly blasphemous—perhaps it was a camouflaged sign of faith), politicians and bureaucrats were to be mocked, and taxmen were to be defied.

Although smuggling had been practised for centuries, it had only been of importance to Llueso and Puerto Llueso from the turn of the century and it had only really flourished after the outbreak of the Civil War. Then, there had been men desperate to disappear before they were taken up into the hills and shot and farmers eager to sell their produce at better prices than those laid down by the authorities. After the end of the war, trade had once more slipped back, but later the tourists had begun to arrive, with so much money it seemed they were all millionaires, and they had demanded goods which either were not normally available or else bore a ridiculous amount of tax. Smuggling had prospered once more.

Prosperity had brought innumerable benefits to what had been a poor island; but such was the nature of all change it had also brought many crosses, of which the worst was undoubtedly drugs.

Hibrero Navarro would never have smuggled drugs. He had been able neither to read nor to write, yet he had known to a hair's-breadth where lay the line which divided right from wrong. But his sons, Miguel and Carlos, were of the next generation, brought up in a time when many men once penniless had become extremely wealthy, and perhaps they had learned to read and write, but because of envy had lost the ability to see where that line lay . . .

Alvarez rang Capitan Reiff who was in charge of the drug squad. Reiff was an arrogant man from the Peninsula (in which he resembled Salas) and so he was careful to speak in Castilian and to sound deferential. 'I'm very sorry to bother you, señor, but I've been wondering if you can help me. Have you made any arrests in the past few days?'

'Why d'you want to know?'

'It's like this. I had a call from a woman in Tarragona whose husband came to the island last Sunday and was supposed to stay at the Hotel Bahia Azul. But when she rang the hotel on Monday morning, they knew nothing about him. She waited, in case something had made him change his mind and he couldn't immediately let her know, but she didn't hear from him and so in the end she got through to me. She's naturally very worried that something's happened to him. I've spoken to the people in the hotel and they say that not only did he never turn up, despite what his wife believes he didn't even make a reservation. Naturally, in case she'd made a mistake about the name of the hotel, I've been in touch with all those in the port . . .'

'Why bother me with this? Probably all that's happened is that he's off with another woman.'

'I hadn't thought of that!

The captain made a sound of derisive contempt.

'I'd best get back on to her and try to find out if she's any suspicions. Of course that'll be a bit tricky. I mean, I don't think I can just come straight out with the suggestion . . .'

'How you go about it is no concern of mine.'

'Of course not, señor . . . there is just one more point. I did wonder if he might have been operating illegally and that's why he gave his wife false information. Have you information on any drugs' movement in the past few days?'

'No.'

'Then I needn't bother you any further, señor. Thank you very much for all your help.' Alvarez replaced the receiver, satisfied that his request for information would be dismissed as witless and not give the capitan cause to wonder if something were going on which he ought to know about . . .

He left the office and drove down to the port, where he parked on the eastern arm of the harbour, close to the harbourmaster's office. Two types of fishing-boats still worked from the port; in-shore and off-shore. The in-shore ones were small and without a wheelhouse, the off-shore ones were slightly larger and had a cramped wheelhouse; as a further sub-division, a couple of the off-shore boats had more powerful diesel engines than the others or than their papers stated. Only one of the two was tied up and a man was aboard her, scrubbing down her stern with a long-handled brush.

'How are things?' Alvarez called out.

Martinez stopped work. He hawked, spat over the side into the scummy water, rested his weight on the handle of the broom.

'Are you busy?'

'Busier'n you.' He was short, squat, and looked as old and battered as his boat; bare to the waist, his chest, where it wasn't covered by a mat of grey hair, was the colour of ancient, muddy bronze.

'But not too busy for a drink, I'll lay?'

'Are you buying?'

'If you're drinking.'

'Why are you buying?'

'Because I'd like the pleasure of a chat with an old friend.'

'If that was all there was to it, you'd want the old friend to do the buying.'

'Come on ashore, you sour old bastard.'

Martinez was reluctant to move, but Alvarez made it clear that he was prepared to wait. Swearing, Martinez brushed a last trickle of water through the nearest scupper, laid the brush down on the deck, picked up a dirty T-shirt which he pulled over his broad shoulders, then jumped ashore with an agility which mocked his years.

'Where d'you like to drink these days?' asked Alvarez.

'Somewhere where I can choose who I drink with.'

'What about Tomi's?'

'Are you now so bloody rich you like paying tourist prices?'

'Tomi's was all right when I was last there.'

'Then it's a long time since you were.' He began to walk.

They reached the road, crossed to the far pavement and continued past shops which catered for foreigners and in which the prices were high, the quality often low, and taste usually non-existent. A side road brought them to a small bar, seldom patronized by tourists since from the outside it looked dirty and it did not serve snacks with chips. Inside it was spotlessly clean and on the walls were framed photographs of the port which showed a small, sleepy fishing village. Alvarez ordered two brandies, carried the glasses over to a table and sat opposite Martinez. 'You and Hibrero were friends, weren't you?'

Martinez produced a cigar and lit it.

'Elena, his mother, is a very distant relation of mine.'

'It always was a bloody unlucky family.'

'She came to the house to tell me that her grandsons are missing and have been since Sunday. Did you see them sail out?'

'No.'

'They should have returned the next morning. She's worried sick, which is hardly surprising since Hibrero died at sea. Shot by the guardia. Wouldn't stop, so they said. If that's true, it meant he reckoned he couldn't ditch the cargo before they came alongside and so he tried to make a run for it. I could never understand why he made such a mistake. If they'd caught him with a cargo, they'd have put him inside for a couple of years, but he'd have lived.'

Martinez slowly considered what had been said and what had been left unsaid; he understood that Alvarez's sympathies lay with Hibrero, not with the law. 'A couple of years be buggered,' he finally said angrily. 'Hibrero thought the guardia a bunch of ignorant Andaluce peasants and when he'd been drinking, which was often enough, he'd taunt them with being so stupid they'd never get within a thousand years of catching him. I've seen him jeering at them until they were redder in the face than a cock's comb. They'd have fixed the evidence to put him away for life.'

'Is that so? . . . If he was smart, which he was, how come they got so close to him when he was on a run?'

'I've just told you, he wasn't so smart after he'd drunk a few.'

'Are you saying that someone informed on him?'

'How else could the guardia have got that close to him?'

'Who talked?'

'If we knew, d'you think the bastard would still be breathing?'

Alvarez picked up the glasses and took them across to the bar to be refilled. Back at the table, he said: 'Before I came down here, I phoned the drug squad in Palma to see if they'd taken Miguel and Carlos in and were holding 'em for questioning.'

'Then you're as bleeding stupid as them. The Navarros have never touched drugs.'

'Hibrero wouldn't have done. But times change and people change with 'em.'

Martinez leaned forward until his stomach was against the edge of the table and said bitterly: 'Haven't you even enough sense to learn that there are people who don't ever change?'

'But are those two some of 'em?'

There was a short silence. Alvarez said: 'If you're so sure of them, tell me where they are now.'

'How would I bloody know?' He sat back, drew on the cigar and let the smoke trickle out of his nose.

'Because you know about everything that goes on around here . . . Elena's wearing black because of her husband and her son. She's terrified that now she's wearing it for both her grandsons as well. She has to know, one way or the other, even if the knowledge will be poison.'

Martinez emptied his glass in two quick swallows and pushed it across the table. Alvarez had both glasses refilled.

Martinez drank, put his glass down on the table. 'Carlos is dead, Miguel is injured.'

'What happened?'

'The boat sank.'

'Why?'

'I don't know.'

'Which hospital is Miguel in?'

'None.'

'Because he was on a run and daren't take the risk of being questioned about how he got his wounds?'

Martinez shrugged his shoulders.

As he drove back from the port to Llueso, Alvarez considered what he's just learned and he wondered how much more Martinez knew but had refused to divulge because he could not, or would not, forget he was speaking to a detective, even if one whose sympathies had been made clear.

Dolores welcomed Alvarez with a torrent of angry words. 'You've finally decided to come home, then! When it suits you and not when I expect you. After all, why should you care what I expect? It means nothing to you that I've spent all day slaving in a kitchen that was hotter than hell, labouring to prepare a delicious supper which needs to be eaten at the right moment. Thoughts like that would never bother you. You tell me you'll be back at such-and-such a time, then return an hour late and the meal's ruined and all my work has been reduced to ashes. Are you in the least bit concerned? Of course not!'

'I'm sorry, but . . .'

She put her hands on her hips and held her head high. 'You say you are sorry, but that is only because I speak. If I were prepared to remain silent, as you'd like, you would not bother to say anything except you wanted your meal now. But you're unlucky. I am not prepared to be quiet.'

'I've been working . . .'

'But of course. And it's only a coincidence—which you regret—that much of your work had to take place in the bars of Llueso and the port.'

'Damnit! I've been finding out about Miguel and Carlos.'

'And for that it is so necessary to drink?'

'Who says I've been drinking?'

'I do.'

'All right. But that was only because I had to have a word with someone.'

'Someone who, no doubt, is incapable of talking outside of a bar?'

'I had to persuade him to tell me what's been going on . . . Carlos is dead.'

'Mother of God!' she whispered, her mood abruptly changed. She went over to the chair next to the one in which Jaime was sitting and slumped down in it. 'Why is life so cruel?' She looked up, her dark brown eyes moist. 'And what about Miguel?'

'He's injured, but I don't know how badly.'

'Then ring the hospital and find out.'

'I can't. He's not in a hospital.'

'Why not? Because he was smuggling when it happened?'

'Yes. So now I have to try and find him and discover how badly injured he is before I go and speak to Elena.'

She nodded. 'If you say he is still alive, she will pray to

all the saints that he recovers and in her heart she will be certain they must listen to her because she is an old woman who has suffered so; but sometimes the saints are deaf and then it will be so much worse for her . . .' She became silent.

'Whoever's looking after him will have made certain that he's very well hidden so that there's no chance the guardia discover he's been injured and start to put two and two together. Has the Navarro family any relations who live in the mountains?'

She thought for a long time, then said: 'There are some distant cousins; an old couple who won't leave their house even though the children have begged and begged them to move somewhere where there are other people to notice if they are in trouble. But where? In God's name, where do the two old people live?'

'Tomaxi,' said Jaime.

She turned and looked at him, astonished that he should remember something that she could not.

CHAPTER 12

Puig Tomaxi was only fifteen kilometres from Llueso, but ten of these kilometres were up in the mountains and by car it was a journey which took at least three-quarters of an hour. Tomaxi was the name of the valley at the head of which stood the puig, a mountain with twin crests, just over a thousand metres high. The valley was narrow and not long and even now the land was heartbreakingly stony despite the past generations of men and women who, day after day, removed stones and built them into walls or stacked them on waste land so poor that not even they had considered it cultivatable. The lower slopes on either side of the valley were steep, but these had been terraced in days when people had never heard about cost-effectiveness.

There was only the one farm in the valley, yet even so the land had never provided the family with more than a bare living. The buildings were grouped together at the far end—the house, with stables attached, and two barns, built of stone, with roofs of bamboos and tiles and without glass in any of the windows, as dourly severe in appearance as the mountains.

As he slowly drove down the road which wound its tortuous way towards the floor of the valley, Alvarez tried to sort out his own mind. If Miguel proved to be in the farmhouse, then there were questions which he must be asked; but what to do about the answers? . . . He and Carlos had been fishermen all their working lives and therefore it was safe to assume that their boat had not been lost through negligence or stupidity. So had it been lost through the action of others? What others? Not the police. Fellow smugglers? But the two brothers were of the traditional smuggling fraternity. Or had they, despite what Martinez had said, tried to break into a trade—drugs—that was far from traditional and which paid so much more than did the normal goods and had someone decided to eliminate their competition? Hibrero would never have smuggled drugs, not for any fortune, but his two sons . . . Alvarez nodded. He now knew what he had to do. If they had been into drugs, then, no matter how cruelly his actions affected Elena and Ana, no matter that they had trusted him and would see his action as an unforgivable betrayal of their trust, he would hand Miguel over to the drug squad. Just as Hibrero had always known where lay the line between what was morally right and what was morally wrong—as opposed to legally—so did he.

He reached the floor of the valley and soon the road deteriorated into a pot-holed dirt track. As the car wallowed on its springs, he wondered how long it would be before this land was abandoned? Only as long as it took the couple to die. Even he, who desired more than anything else in the world a finca of his own, would not try to farm here. All that this land produced successfully was despair.

He parked in front of the house and walked across the bone-dry, cracked earth. He was half way to the door when a man stepped out. 'Manolo Caceres?' he asked. Caceres was old and almost as dried-up as the land, yet Alvarez could be certain that he still did a day's work that would shame most townsmen. 'My name's Enrique Alvarez; I'm a cousin of Dolores Ramez, who's a cousin of Elena Navarro.'

'Cousin Inspector Alvarez,' sneered Caceres.

That he had been identified enabled Alvarez to guess what had happened. The previous evening, Martinez had defended the sons of his old friend and had vehemently denied there could be the slightest possibility they had moved from traditional smuggling into drugs. But afterwards, knowing how greed had changed many Mallorquins, he'd begun to wonder and the more he'd wondered, the less certain he'd become . . . But Hibrero had been his friend and until he could know the truth beyond doubt, he owed Hibrero's remaining son the duty forged by that friendship and so he had passed word through that Miguel had to be moved in case the Inspector was bright enough to work out where he was likely to be hiding . . . 'Miguel's not here any longer, is he?'

No answer.

'When did he leave—late last night?'

No answer.

'Where's he been moved to?'

No answer.

Alvarez brought a pack of cigarettes from his pocket and offered it. Caceres stared into the distance. Alvarez lit a cigarette. 'Elena's going crazy with worry.'

A woman called out: 'Who is it?' A moment later, she appeared in the doorway. She was the same age as her husband, but looked even older because her back was so badly bowed from decades of working bent double in the fields.

'It's Cousin Inspector Alvarez,' sneered Caceres.

Alvarez spoke to her. 'I'm here to try and help Elena. She doesn't know where Miguel and Carlos are and she's terrified that something's happened to them and she has to mourn afresh. I know that Carlos is dead, but do I have also to tell her that Miguel may die so that she will be left without grandsons?'

'It's in God's hands.'

'Be quiet, woman,' Caceres shouted.

'How badly injured is he?' asked Alvarez.

She ignored her husband's order. 'He has broken ribs, burns, and many bad bruises.'

'What happened?'

'He'd gone up to the front of the boat and there was an explosion which threw him against the side. If he'd been near Carlos, he'd have died also.'

'What caused the explosion?'

Caceres shouted: 'There wasn't one. The wife's talking stupidities. We've seen no one and we know nothing.' He swung round and spoke angrily to his wife, his words inaudible to Alvarez. She returned into the house. He ordered Alvarez to leave, every other word an obscenity.

Alvarez returned to his car and drove back along the pot-holed track. An explosion aboard a diesel-engined fishing-boat which almost certainly had not been carrying bottled gas surely suggested a bomb, planted by men determined to get rid of two newcomers to the drug trade?

He had thought of a way in which he could avoid having personally to tell Elena that one grandson was dead and the other injured, but because it had become his duty to deliver this tragic message, he rejected the temptation to any such evasion. But when he drove up to Elena's house it was to discover that only Ana was at home, looking tired and careworn; the crying of the baby suggested at least part of the reason for this.

'Grandmother's not here,' she said abruptly.

Initially, he was surprised, having imagined that Elena would not have moved from the house until he returned to tell her if he'd managed to learn anything. 'D'you know where she is?'

'She . . . she went into Palma to shop.'

Ana was not a good liar; or perhaps she was too tired and worried to try to sound sincere. He realized that he'd been rather naïve to be surprised by Elena's absence. Word had reached her that Miguel was alive, but injured, and she had gone to nurse him. Alvarez said quietly: 'They say that Miguel's injured, but it sounds as if he's not critically ill.'

Tears trickled down her cheeks as she began to sob; in her grief, she looked ugly, the worst features of her face being exaggerated and the better ones obscured. With an unthinking gesture of appeal, she reached out for him and he hugged her to himself as he murmured comforting words and assured her everything would be all right in the end, even as he hated himself for being such a hypocrite since soon he might have to arrest Miguel.

Her emotions calmed and she quickly drew away from him, suddenly embarrassed by the embrace. He said: 'When I need a bit of help to face the world, I have a drink. Perhaps you're the same?'

She hesitated.

'Where will I find something?'

She led the way into the room with the suite of furniture in white leather and pointed to the heavily carved sideboard. The baby's cries intensified and she hurried out of the room, returning with him in her arms. Alvarez opened the doors of the sideboard and he couldn't remember seeing a larger selection of drinks in a private home. Yet another indication that the brothers had been making far more money than conventional smuggling had ever offered? . . . She said she'd have the same as he, a brandy, and he searched among the bottles, quickly finding a Torres Gran Reserva. 'Where are the glasses?'

'In the kitchen.'

He followed her. The walls of the kitchen needed retiling, the ceiling needed repainting, and the floor was plain concrete, yet the gas stove was large and new, on the working surfaces was every possible kind of electrical machine, and the refrigerator was a very large two-door model with an ice dispenser.

They sat outside, at the battered wooden patio table, shaded by the overhead vine whose fruit was formed but stone hard.

'What have you heard about Miguel's condition?' he asked.

She did not bother to try to make out that she had heard nothing. 'He will recover.' She stroked the baby's head. 'I told them not to,' she said suddenly.

'Not to do what?' he asked, judging she was far too wrapped up in her fears, doubts, and tiredness, to realize that she needed to guard her tongue.

'I said I was scared because nothing ever comes so easily, but Carlos just laughed. I said at least to save some of the money and not to spend it all, but Carlos called me an idiot because when he needed more, he'd get it.'

'They'd found something new to smuggle?'

She did not answer him. 'Carlos said I was always preaching disaster. But I know that nothing ever comes easily, except trouble.'

'When was all this happening?'

'Recently,' she said vaguely. 'When he bought the furniture and the stuff in the kitchen and the new bed for grandmother, the car, and the christening robe for Pedro . . .' She stared down at her son with a look of love and fear. 'I said to Carlos, Pedro could be christened in the robe I was. He wouldn't hear of that; said mine wasn't nearly good enough for a Navarro and so he went into Palma and bought one that cost fifty thousand. Fifty thousand!

'When I saw it and he told me how much he'd paid, I was frightened. I mean, we're only ordinary people and if we start behaving like we're more, then . . .' She struggled, but failed, to find the words to express her instinctive fear that the gods always punished pretensions. 'Carlos laughed at me—sometimes Miguel went for him for doing that, but he didn't care. He said . . .' The baby began to grizzle and she jogged him up and down in her arms. 'D'you think it could be more teeth coming through?'

'I wouldn't know.'

'I don't think it can be. But I'm sure he hasn't eaten anything nasty . .'

'What did Carlos say?'

'The robe came floating down from heaven, so it was the luckiest robe any baby could possibly wear to a christening. He's always teasing me. So sometimes I tease him back and ask him when he's going to marry his novia . . .' She suddenly remembered that he would never tease her again, never laugh at her again, and never buy her another fifty-thousand peseta robe. She began to cry and the tears slid down her cheeks and fell on to Pedro, who prodded the sudden dampness with inquiring fingers. She wept for her husband and for her brother-in-law, and because life could be kind one moment and yet so cruel the next.

Alvarez went through to the kitchen to find that Dolores was vigorously working a pestle in a mortar. She stopped, straightened up, rubbed the sweat from her forehead with the back of her hand. 'Well?'

'Elena has gone to care for Miguel and so I didn't see her. I don't think Ana knows where she's gone.'

'So what will happen now?'

'I just don't know.' By which he meant that he couldn't be certain enough that Miguel and Carlos had moved from traditional smuggling to drug-running and, being something of a coward who would face a moral dilemma when forced to, but who far preferred not to be so forced, he was very glad that that was so.

CHAPTER 13

Alvarez slowly climbed the stairs and went along to his office. He sat, breathing heavily and sweating profusely. He must, he decided, cut back on smoking and drinking. Then he thought about life and he reached down to the bottom right-hand drawer of the desk and brought out from this the bottle of brandy and a glass. He was in the middle of the drink when the phone rang.

'Robert here. How are things your end? But please don't tell me you're so hot you don't know what to do. Here the calendar may say it's August, but it's damn near freezing and if it doesn't rain before the day's out, I'll eat my hat.'

'My trouble is not the heat, it's the amount of work.'

Ware laughed. 'If I didn't know you, I might sympathize . . . I'm phoning because I promised to keep you up to date with the news. Something odd's happened. Serena Collins, sole beneficiary under Green's will, has instructed solicitors to claim against his life insurance. As you know, I'd have given odds on that after she'd passed on my message they'd come to the conclusion they'd better forget the claim because if they didn't he'd be for the high jump on a charge of attempted fraud.'

'He cannot believe that your company is in as strong a position as you made out.'

'Or he's so desperate for money that he's willing to take the gamble that he can successfully keep out of sight. His scenario must go like this. She puts in a claim, the company refuses to pay so she takes them to court and since nothing's completely certain at law, maybe she wins, because her lawyers are clever, maybe she loses, because the company's are cleverer. If she loses and it's impossible legally to tie her up directly with the intended fraud, she avoids any criminal action against herself . . . But he's got to be really desperate. After all, they can't be certain how strong our case is and we may easily have dug up more evidence than I told her about. And once the court learns how closely she's been associated with Green, to the extent that she was waiting for him in the flat in Changres, had rung up his hotel in Mallorca, knowing he was flying, isn't it going to be very difficult for her to claim she had no knowledge of all that was going on? . . . I know, I'm going round in circles and arguing against myself, but frankly I can't make sense of their action. And that's got me worried that I've missed something or that something fresh has happened which had tipped the scales in their favour. I suppose you've nothing fresh to add?'

'I'm afraid not.'

'Then I'll just have to go on worrying and grow ever bigger ulcers.'

When the call was over, Alvarez finished the drink, replaced bottle and glass in the drawer—enjoying a glow of congratulatory self-satisfaction as he did so because he had resisted the temptation to pour himself a second drink. He settled back in the chair and watched a fly walk across one of the folders which littered the desk. Greed, although not one of the deadly sins, was certainly one of the deadliest to those who suffered it. It was greed which had made Green try to double the sum insured, an act which had raised the suspicion of fraud; it was greed which was persuading him to pursue the claim, through the señorita, an act which might well prove fatal to them both . . .

He was on the point of falling asleep when a memory, which he couldn't immediately identify, irritatingly jerked him awake. Had Dolores asked him to buy something on his way home? He couldn't begin to remember her doing so. And in any case, this elusive memory seemed to be somehow connected with something Ware had said. He thought back to their conversation. Ware was afraid that he'd missed something or that something had happened which had tipped the scales in favour of Green. But how could either possibility be . . . Ana! She'd been given a fifty-thousand peseta christening robe and when she'd expressed her worry at such ostentatious munificence, Carlos had laughed at her fears and said that it had to be the luckiest of robes because it had floated down from heaven. It was an extraordinary thing for a man like him to say if it were mere persiflage; poetic images would never rush to his lips. So could it have been said with jeering irony; had he and Miguel been out on either a fishing trip or a smuggling run, seen a parachute descend, watched the parachutist board a motor-cruiser which had headed north, and then later learned that the pilot of the plane was supposed to have died in the crash? They'd recognize a smart fraud when they saw one. And they'd know that they could expect to make themselves a great deal of money by blackmail. But perhaps what they hadn't realized was that they were moving out of their class. Green was never going to permit his elaborate fraud to be wrecked by two fishermen. He'd planted a bomb on their boat which had been intended to blast both of them into silence . . .

If he were right, then the newfound wealth of the brothers didn't mean they'd moved into drugs. Which in turn meant he would not have to arrest Miguel and subsequently face Elena's and Ana's stunned incomprehension and Dolores's anger . . . For the moment he chose to ignore the fact that if Miguel had been party to an attempted blackmail, then he had been guilty of a serious crime, even if the man being blackmailed was a criminal . . .

Alvarez braked the car to a halt in front of the elaborate wrought-iron gates and as he climbed out of the car he wondered how much just this gateway had cost? Ca'n Feut represented a degree of wealth that he'd not met before and he found it impossible to visualize the kind of life that Bennett must lead. Did he think like an ordinary person? Could he, if he was in a position to buy virtually anything he wanted without a second's thought? Did he ever look beyond his wealth and see a world in which there was so much want? Did he ever stop to wonder if eventually he would be called upon to pay a price for all the privileges he had enjoyed?

He pressed the red button on the speaker box and when the call was answered he identified himself and asked if Señor Bennett was at home. Just before he returned to the car, he looked up at the TV camera and suffered a childish desire to stick out his tongue . . .

The gates opened and he drove up the winding road to the crown of the hill. The lawn was the same shade of dark green—a minimum of a lorry-load of water a day. And yet he knew farmers in the area who could no longer irrigate their land and grow crops in the summer because in order to maintain the tourist trade the extraction of water had become so great that the water-table had fallen to the point where their wells ran dry. He was the least vindictive of men, but he knew he would not be dismayed if one day there were no water lorries to climb the hill and the flowers withered and the grass died back and Bennett discovered that all the wealth in the world could never divorce a man from that world.

He stepped out of the car and then turned back and leaned over to pick up from the passenger seat the small folded yachting chart which he'd borrowed from the harbourmaster. He crossed to the front door and rang the bell. The door was opened by a young woman and he politely wished her good-morning.

'You don't remember me?'

She was the second person in a short time whom he'd

failed to recognize. They said that loss of memory was the first sign of approaching senility . . .

'I'm Cristina.'

'Not Julián's daughter?'

'That's right.'

'Well, I'm damned!' He was reassured that senility had not yet crept all that close. The last time he'd seen her, she'd worn glasses, her face had been spotty, and she'd been very shy. He recalled the old Mallorquin proverb: Time works miracles for the young and tragedies for the old. 'How can you expect me to recognize you when you've grown so beautiful since I last saw you?'

She simpered at the compliment.

'What exactly are you doing here?'

'Working about the house, cleaning and that sort of thing, and helping Juana in the kitchen.'

'I met her last time I was here.'

'She told me. It was my day off.'

'Is it a good job?'

'Not so bad except when it's Juana's day off and I have to do everything. Still, at least I don't have to do the cooking now—just take something out of the deep-freeze and warm it up for the señor.' She laughed gaily. 'At the start, he said I was to do the cooking on her day off, but when I did, he soon changed his mind!'

'Clever! . . . I suppose I'd better go and have a word with the señor. Is he on his own?'

'At the moment, but he's expecting a señorita.'

'Then I'd better be brief if I'm not to spoil his pleasures.'

She giggled, then led the way through the hall and the sitting-room on to the pool patio.

Bennett, wearing a costume, sat by a table in the centre of which was fixed a sun umbrella, but his chair was set clear of the shade. On the table was an ice-bucket in which was a bottle of champagne and by its side a half-filled flute.

'Good morning, señor.'

'More questions?'

'I'm afraid I have to ask a few more.'

'Then as quickly as you can. I have a guest due soon.'

There were three other chairs around the table; since Bennett said nothing, he moved one of them into the shade and sat. The bottle of champagne was close and when he spoke he was conscious of how dry was his throat. 'Señor, on the thirteenth of last month you sailed from the port in your boat.'

'I answered the last time you were here that I have no idea.'

'And you sailed at four-thirty in the afternoon.'

'Why this absurd—'

'Señor, I hope you will understand my questions in a moment and begin to remember.'

Bennett's expression tightened.

'How fast is your boat?'

'I'm tempted to answer, how long is a piece of string? . . . Do you mean maximum, cruising, or manœuvring speed?'

'The speed at which you sail on a long journey.'

'Cruising. Twelve knots.'

'Why did you sail for Stivas in the afternoon, which meant that you had to spend the night at sea?'

He no longer denied remembering. 'I wanted to.'

'Because you needed the dark?'

'That question suggests you're continuing to make the same absurd accusations as last time.' He picked the bottle out of the ice-bucket and topped up his drink.

The champagne was Krug. Nothing so common as Codorníu's Non Plus Ultra, thought Alvarez, as he tried very hard not to imagine the velvety pleasure of ice-cold champagne slipping down his parched throat. He stood, put the chart on the table, and unfolded it. 'I would like to show you something, señor.' He brought a pair of dividers out of his pocket, removed the cork with which he had protected the points, measured from the latitude scale twelve minutes. A course from Puerto Llueso, rounding Cabo Parelona, to Stivas had been laid off and along this he measured six and a half hours' run with the dividers. He marked the spot with a small cross in pencil. 'This is where your boat was at eleven o'clock that night.'

'Really.'

'Do you see this other mark, señor?'

Bennett briefly stared down at the chart. 'Yes.'

'That is where the plane was when the last radio message was sent. The two positions are close together.'

'Before you try to draw the slightest significance from that fact, let me point out something. If I steered even a slightly different course from the one you have decided that I did—on no evidence at all, as far as I'm aware—if my speed over the ground was slightly more or less than twelve knots because of a current or engine revs, or a dozen other variables were in operation, my position was many miles distant from where you've plotted it.'

'All that is possible, but what is fact is that you were in a position to pick up the pilot after he had parachuted from the plane.'

'I wonder if anything I can say will ever bring home to you the stupidity of the accusation?'

Alvarez placed his finger on the chart. 'When you were there, were there any other craft around?'

'Wherever I was at eleven that night, there were no other vessels in sight.'

'Can you be certain, since it was dark?'

'All vessels at sea carry steaming lights. And you have, perhaps, heard of radar?'

'Of course, señor, and I believe your boat has a set. Would this have picked up a fishing-boat?'

'If you were at all conversant with the subject, you'd again know that I'd need more information before I could answer. At what range was such boat, what was her size and shape, of what was she constructed, were there any cliffs behind her to mask the blip or obscure it with reflected scatter?'

'Then what you're really saying is that a fishing-boat might have observed you even though you had no idea it was there?'

'I still can't answer. If someone aboard this mythical craft could see my steaming lights (and how else would that person have known of my presence?) I would have expected to pick her up on my radar unless she lay very low in the water and had a very poor radar profile.'

'I imagine that the lights you had to burn to guide the parachuting pilot down and to show him exactly where the surface of the sea lay would have been visible at a greater distance than any normal lights?'

Bennett lifted his glass and drained it, then checked his gold Audemars-Piguet. 'Without wishing to appear rude, I do hope you've nearly reached the end of all these absurd questions since, as I said, I'm expecting a guest?'

'I've only a few more, señor, and I'll ask those as quickly as possible. Did Green parachute from his plane into the sea and did you pick him up?'

'If you haven't already gathered what my answer is to that ridiculous question, I think you must find your present job an onerous one.'

'What do you say when I tell you that two fishermen saw you pick up a parachutist?'

'That they were probably tight.'

'We have traced the hotel in Stivas where Señor Green stayed on the Sunday night under the name of Thomas Grieves. And I think that now he has returned to the island.'

'In view of the fact that he's dead, I can only applaud your imagination; it's not given to everyone easily to envisage a second coming.'

'You do realize something, do you, señor?'

'If you are postulating it, I doubt that I do.'

'When you sailed Señor Green to the Peninsula, you became an accomplice to attempted fraud; if you know he is back on this island, but deny the fact, you may well become an accessory after the fact to murder.'

Bennett refilled his glass. Alvarez carefully stared out at the magnificent view, but for once failed to gain any sense of pleasure from it.

Bennett said, as he replaced the bottle in the ice-bucket: 'I do wonder if something has occurred to you. If Green faked the crash and I sailed him to the mainland, his objective must have been to get as far away from here as possible. He's hardly likely, then, to have returned.' He drank.

'There are times when the best hiding-place is where a person is known to have fled from, since no one will believe he could be so stupid as to return.'

'You are clearly a man of great ingenuity as well as imagination.'

Alvarez stood. 'Thank you for your help, señor.'

Bennett nodded. He could have been smiling slightly, but it was impossible to be certain.

Alvarez was half way to the house when the sitting-room door opened and a woman stepped out. She was neatly dressed, but not stylishly, certainly not in her youth, and pleasant-looking rather than pretty. He was surprised. He'd have thought that only an exotic woman would have attracted Bennett. As she drew level with him she smiled a greeting and he inclined his head.

'Hullo, Serena,' Bennett called out.

''Morning, Pat. It's even hotter than ever, isn't it?'

She'd a warm voice, thought Alvarez; the kind a man liked to hear when he returned home after a hard day's work. He went to open the door into the sitting-room, but it was opened for him by Cristina. He stepped into the cool room. 'I meant to ask you how your mother is? The last time I saw her, she was having a lot of trouble with her back.'

'It's not got any better and none of the doctors seem to be able to do any good for her.'

'I'm sorry to hear that. Will you give her my best wishes?'

'Yes, of course I will.'

They entered the hall. He jerked his thumb behind himself. 'Not the most friendly type, is he?'

'Him! When he speaks to the likes of us, his words are covered with ice.'

He said goodbye to her and left the house. There was a white Seat 127 parked behind his car and on the rear nearside window of this was the form which every hire-car had to show. So the señorita was a tourist. Serena. Not a common name, he judged, and yet he had only recently come across it . . . He came to a stop, turned, hurried back to the door and rang the bell. When Cristina opened it, he said: 'Can you tell me the surname of the señorita who's just arrived?'

'She told me what it was when she phoned before she came up here the first time. What was it?' She frowned. 'I know it sounded like someone who's on the telly . . .'

'Collins?'

'How ever did you guess?'

CHAPTER 14

As Alvarez waited for Salas to come on the line, he heard a screech of brakes from the road, but for once this was not followed by the thump of one car hitting another. Most of Llueso had been built when mule carts had been the only form of transport and the narrow, twisted streets and the large stones sunk into the ground at every corner to prevent the carts' wheels from scoring the walls, reflected that fact.

Now, Mallorquin drivers, who so often saw themselves as matadors of the wheel, bumped into each other with expensive monotony.

Salas said: 'What is it?'

'I'm ringing about the Green case, señor. There's reason to think he may be on the island.'

'Surely it's only very recently that you assured me he was in eastern France?'

'That is one of the reasons why I think he may well be here.'

'Alvarez, can you appreciate that there is a certain lack of logic in what you'd just said?'

'I know it may sound a bit like that . . . I suppose you could call it a paradox.'

'I doubt I would. I'd have thought that experience had finally and painfully left me incapable of being surprised by anything you might do or say. I would be wrong.'

'It's because anyone with even a gramme of common sense would be certain that he'll keep as far away as possible, since he might be recognized which would make it all too clear he's not dead, that I reckon he's chosen to return.'

'You are saying, in effect, that you lack that gramme of common sense?'

'I'm saying, señor, that this is the one place where he will know we'll be most unlikely to look for him now we've confirmed that his death was faked.'

'Even if it does make—according to you—for a possible hiding-place, there are very many safer. So why should he have returned?'

This was the question he had feared. To answer correctly and say that Green had returned to murder the Navarro brothers was to expose Miguel to the charge that he had been drug-running; as yet, there was no proof of his innocence; quite the reverse, really, since the circumstantial evidence against him was so strong that he'd find it very difficult to prove his innocence. The case had developed such complications . . . 'Señor, I cannot yet give a decisive answer. But Serena Collins, the woman who is his accomplice, is on the island.'

'From which you deduce what?'

'That she is here to be close to him.'

'An even riskier move. How did you discover she was here?'

'It was because . . .' He stopped as he realized that once again he could hardly explain that he'd been pursuing inquiries aimed at clearing Miguel. 'Because I wanted another word with Bennett,' he said lamely.

'Why?'

'Something about his evidence worried me, but I couldn't pin it down.'

'Worried you in what way?'

'Frankly, I don't really know . . . I'm sorry, señor, but I'm afraid I'm not very good at explaining myself.'

'Perhaps you are presenting yourself with an impossible task.'

'Señor, we know that Green is using a false passport in the name of Thomas Grieves, but he won't know that we know and all he'll know is . . .'

'For God's sake, man, do try not to confuse the matter any further.'

'Yes, señor. I'd like to ask for a check on all airlines and the ferries to see if Thomas Grieves entered the island on or before last Sunday and with all hotels and hostals to see if he's presently booked in at any of them.'

'And all that simply because you're worried about something Bennett may or may not have said?'

'Because Señorita Collins is on the island. We mustn't forget that we were asked by England to give all possible assistance to Señor Ware. If they should learn that Green is here now, but we don't know where he is, they might think us rather incompetent.'

'As to that, their conclusions would undoubtedly depend

on whom they spoke to,' snapped Salas, before he bad-temperedly agreed to the request and rang off.

Alvarez drove past the No Entry sign and parked. He left the car and walked down to the front. The sandy beach was packed with sunbathers, the colour of their bodies ranging from white, through red, to brown; off-shore, several ski boats were churning white wakes and beyond them were yachts, with multi-colour spinnakers, ghosting along in the very light breeze; a firefighting seaplane dipped down in the middle of the bay and skimmed the surface, then rose with a sheet of water cascading from its hull as it began its short flight to a point where a fire, almost certainly set by an arsonist, was burning. He remembered his first sight of the bay—almost no sand on the beaches, perhaps half a dozen bathers, no power boats. Then, there had been peace as well as beauty. The peace had vanished, much of the beauty still remained. But how long before that was gone as well, banished by the press of people who sought it? It was acknowledged wisdom that one should never look back. Acknowledged wisdom did not go on to suggest how one avoided doing just that.

Along the front were a number of hotels and he entered the first he came to, one which had recently been converted into a number of self-catering units. He asked the young man at the reception desk whether a Señorita Collins was registered. The receptionist checked and said that no, they had no one by that name staying with them. He left.

The front road at this point was closed to traffic other than buses, cars, and taxis, picking up or putting down passengers, and the sight of people drinking at the outside tables made him very thirsty, but the knowledge of the prices charged kept him walking—there was no Ware to pick up the tab. He came to the Regina, a hotel that was family run and which, even though most of its trade was with package tour operators, still offered courteous service.

Two men were behind the desk, the receptionist and the concierge. The younger, the receptionist, said he'd find out whether Señorita Collins was staying at the hotel and he began to check through the registration book while the concierge, who knew Alvarez slightly, began to explain how difficult life was for a man who had his eighty-one-year-old mother—for whom nothing was ever right—living with him. The receptionist interrupted the monologue of complaints. 'We've a señorita of that name staying here.'

'Is she in?' Alvarez asked.

He checked the keys. 'It doesn't look like it.'

'Right. Thanks.'

'D'you want to get in touch with her?' asked the concierge, his curiosity aroused.

'Yes, but don't bother her. I'll come back later.'

'I hope there's nothing wrong? She's a really nice person.'

'Nice, but long in the tooth,' said the receptionist.

The concierge spoke scornfully. 'He reckons that anyone over twenty-five has one foot in the grave.'

'He'll learn that life favours fifty.' Alvarez left and as he walked back to his car he reflected that concierges saw so much of human nature they were left with few illusions, yet the other had said what a nice person Serena Collins was. Ware had said the same thing. Clearly, she was a clever woman who knew how to manipulate susceptible men. It was her misfortune that soon she was going to come up against a man who would prove to be totally unsusceptible to her charms.

Alvarez ate the last slice of banana and two baked almonds. He reached across the table for the bottle of wine and refilled his glass. 'I'll be off in a minute.'

'You're going out now?' said Dolores, surprised.

'I have to have a word with someone down in the port; she wasn't at the hotel earlier on.'

Jaime, who'd been about to drink, put down the glass.

'She's a foreigner? One of . . .' He began to outline a shape with his hands, but stopped when Dolores glared at him.

'One of what?' asked Juan.

'Never you mind,' snapped Dolores. 'And since we've finished, except for those who can't stop drinking, you can start clearing the table.'

'Why have I got to do it?'

'Because I told you to.'

'Why can't Isabel . . .'

'She did it yesterday. If there's any more argument from you, you'll do the clearing the whole of next week.'

Juan, a rebellious look on his face, collected up the plates as clumsily as he dared. Isabel jeered at him and he called her a name which made her cry out with rage and then inform her mother of what had just been said. He stoutly denied the allegation before inadvisedly adding that he'd never heard the word before.

Alvarez left the house and drove down to the port; he parked in front of the Regina. The concierge had returned home and only the night receptionist was at the desk. He turned and looked at the numbered boxes. 'The señorita's key isn't here, so she must be in the hotel.'

'Will you try her room and if you get through say that Inspector Alvarez is here and would like a word with her.'

There was no answer to the call. 'She's maybe still in the dining-room or having coffee outside. Shall I find out?'

'Thanks, but I'll look for myself.'

The dining-room overlooked the bay and the favoured tables were those next to the windows; she was sitting at the corner one. He began to cross the room, threading his way between the tables, when the head waiter stopped him and demanded to know what he wanted in a tone which reminded him that he had forgotten to change his shirt that morning and it was some time since his trousers had boasted a crease. 'Cuerpo General de Policia. I want a word with Señorita Collins.'

The head waiter's manner became very correct and courteous. 'The señorita is over at that table, seated by herself.' He led the way across.

'Miss Collins?' Alvarez asked in English. He introduced himself.

She studied him, then said: 'We've met before, haven't we? You were at Patrick's place earlier on.'

He had expected her eyes to be hard, but they were large and brown and all he could see in them was warmth. 'Yes, I was.'

'And you want to speak to me now?'

'If you don't mind.'

'But what on earth about?' She smiled briefly. 'But you can hardly tell me without speaking, can you? Look, I've finished eating so it's time for coffee. Let's go outside and have it there.'

Outside the hotel there was a space, covered overhead, of about three metres before the pavement and here tables and chairs had been set out for guests. Two were vacant and she chose the nearer one. Once settled, she said: 'I love sitting out here at night. I don't think I've seen anywhere more lovely.'

'And it used to be even more beautiful.'

'Before all we nasty tourists arrived? Sometimes it must be awful, seeing strangers take over your land and changing it so. But there are some compensations, aren't there?'

'A few.'

'But you'd cheerfully forgo them all if time could be turned back?'

Honesty compelled him to say: 'I don't know.'

'It's really one of those unanswerable questions, isn't it, not least because one knows time can't be turned back . . . How wonderful to be rich and noble in the old days and to have every wish tended to by an army of servants; but that's to forget the toothache which drove one half-mad and the appendicitis that was a death warrant. As someone once said, happiness is accepting life as it is, not as it was or will be.'

A waiter came up to the table and she said: 'What would you like?'

'Allow me, señorita. I will have coffee solo; do you prefer it like that or con leche. And perhaps you will have a coñac?'

'Coffee with milk, please, but I don't think I'll have a brandy.'

He spoke in Mallorquin and ordered two coffees and one brandy. The waiter left. 'Señorita, I . . .'

'I've been told that it's always Christian names on this island; mine is Serena.'

'Yes, I know.'

'But you obviously prefer to keep things on a formal footing?' She studied him, a slight frown on her forehead. 'Why? Have you decided you don't like me?'

'It's not my position either to like or dislike you.'

'How boring!' She rested her elbows on the table and her chin on the upturned palms of her hands. 'You should know something. I can read people's true characters, however hard they try to conceal them. That is because my mother came from La Verry, in France. Have you ever heard of the village?'

'No.'

'Verry is a corruption of *vérité*. The town was given its original name in the sixteenth century because some of the women claimed to be able to see the truth that lay in men's hearts. The Church objected to the idea, perhaps on grounds of self-interest, and held that such women were bewitched; several were burned at the stake. But even that dreadful fate couldn't stop the gifts from being handed down through the generations, albeit for a time they were unwelcome and feared gifts. My mother traced her ancestry back to the sister of one of the poor women burned at the stake in fifteen-sixty-one; that is why I can see people for who they really are and not for who they would like others to think them.'

She had spoken quickly and almost recklessly, as if careless about the quality of her words; he thought that this was because she was so eager to distract him from the reason which had brought him to the hotel.

She continued: 'So I can be certain that far from the stern, hard-faced man you wish to present, in truth you are warm-hearted, compassionate, and friendly. Admit it—am I not right?'

'I wouldn't know.'

'You're embarrassed to have your good points exposed? You'd rather be vilified as someone ice-cold and heartless?'

He had to smile.

'That's better! I'll tell you something more about yourself. You should smile much more often; although, of course, it's a complete give-away. When you smile, no widow will ever believe she's about to be turned out from hearth and home.'

'Señorita . . .'

'Again? Despite all I've said?'

'I'm afraid that my visit is an official one so it is necessary to be formal.'

Her expression changed and she looked past him, as if vainly seeking a way of escape.

'I must ask you certain questions.'

'About what?'

'Señor Green.'

She nibbled her lower lip. 'I . . . I can't tell you anything about what happened.'

'I believe that you can.'

She opened her handbag, with some urgency, brought out a silver cigarette case and lighter, and lit a cigarette. Only then did she think to offer him one by pushing the case into the middle of the table. She stared out across the road at the beach.

'Whereabouts on the island is Señor Green now?' he asked quietly.

'He's dead.'

'He is not dead and you know that he is not.'

'Oh God! . . . I'm not nearly as clever as I thought. If you can talk like that, I couldn't begin to see the truth in you. Warm-hearted, compassionate, friendly? You're beastly cruel.'

She stood and left so suddenly that by the time he had come to his feet she was well clear of the table. He watched her go into the hotel, then sat once more. It had been a very difficult part to play and she had not been quite good enough an actress to play it successfully; at the beginning she had been too determinedly carefree, at the end unable to shed tears when these were called for.

The waiter brought the coffee and the brandy. Alvarez slit open both packets of sugar and poured the contents into one cup. He sipped the brandy. He wished that he weren't such an emotional fool that now he felt guilty because he'd forced her to realize that the attempt to fake Green's death had failed. He wondered how much more guilty he would feel if—or was it really when?—he had to convince her that Green had murdered in order to try to preserve the fraud?

CHAPTER 15

Dolores looked across the kitchen. 'What's the matter, Enrique?'

He jerked his attention back to the present and the bowl of hot chocolate and the large slice of coca in front of himself. He crumbled some of the coca and dropped the pieces into the chocolate. 'Nothing.'

'But you've not spoken for ages and have been staring into space.'

'I was thinking.'

'About what?'

'Nothing, really.'

'About a woman?'

'No. At least, not in the way you're thinking.'

'Does a man think of a woman in any other way?'

'My problem is, how do women think about men?'

'That's none of your business.'

'But it is. How would you react if I told you that Jaime had either found or paid a woman to dress in a garter belt, black stockings, and long black boots, and to whip him?'

Her expression was shocked. 'Not Jaime,' she whispered.

Belatedly, he realized that she had misunderstood him. 'Good God, I'm not suggesting that Jaime could ever do anything like that.'

Her shock turned to relief, her relief to anger. 'How dare you mention such disgusting things! If you were Juan, I'd scrub your mouth out with bleach.'

'If I were Juan, I wouldn't yet know enough to ask such a question . . . But this sort of thing goes on.'

'Perhaps. But I don't wish to hear about it.'

'In my job, unfortunately I can't get rid of something by simply refusing to hear about it . . . Please help me. I'm asking you because you're so normal and nice.'

At this compliment, her expression of angry distaste lessened slightly.

'If I had said that Jaime had asked a woman to do that, would you believe me?'

'Never!'

'Yet when I first mentioned it, you immediately thought . . .'

'Be quiet. You've no idea what I thought.'

'All right, I'll accept that. But try and believe it was possible. Would you then do what you could to understand why it had happened?'

'Never!'

'Would you forgive him?'

'Never!'

'If it were not repeated, would you forget?'

'Never!' she exclaimed for the fourth time, even more forcefully than before.

'Not if it wasn't his fault because his desires were so great they were beyond his control?'

'No man's desires are beyond his control. If he acts like a beast, it's because he wishes to be a beast.'

'Just for the moment, I won't argue over that . . .'

'There is no argument.'

'Then suppose a woman can't hide the truth from herself and so she has to accept the fact that her man has got another woman to whip him; but she can forgive and forget. How would you describe such a woman?'

'As one without shame.'

'And perhaps as a woman who might prove to be not all that adverse to administering a whipping?'

'Enrique, how can you say such filthy things in this house?'

'Because I need to be able to judge whether she is deliberately blind, extraordinarily forgiving, or as perverted as he.'

'I know nothing about any of that. I only know that your superior chief should be told that he has no right to ask you to handle so disgusting a case.'

He nodded, as if agreeing with her, spooned some of the sodden coca out of the chocolate and ate it. He accepted that she had expressed her feelings exactly and was grateful for her help. But he recognized that she had lived all her life in a small, narrow-minded community to which outside ideas had only recently reached and her reactions were those of someone to whom moral right and wrong had been sharply defined by background and upbringing. It could be different for someone who came from a sophisticated milieu and had been conditioned since birth to accept that there were occasions or circumstances when for some, yet not for others, moral right and wrong could have different boundaries or even none to separate them, that judgements had to be partially objective and not wholly subjective.

He left the house ten minutes later and drove to the bottom of Calle Juan Rives, turned right, and almost immediately right again which brought him to one of the bridges across the torrente which, at this time of the year, was dry and a handy dumping ground for rubbish. Beyond the bridge was the Laraix road which led into the main Llueso/Puerto Llueso road.

He reached the Navarros' finca and as he braked to a halt he saw a figure working in the field. He shielded his eyes with his hand and recognized Elena. In that case, Miguel must either be out of danger or dead.

He left the car and walked between rows of French beans, then staked tomatoes—although still growing bush varieties, more and more people were staking them—to where she was using a mattock to plug and unplug the irrigation channels. 'Everything's looking even better than before.'

'It'll do,' she answered, using words which tradition decreed since they did not offend the gods, either through presumption or ingratitude.

'Does your being back here mean that Miguel is better?'

She was wearing a wide-brimmed straw hat; she turned her head until she could look up at him and her expression was worried because she could not decide how best to answer the question.

He said: 'Watch the water.'

The main irrigation channel was wide and it allowed a flow of water strong enough to flood a side channel in a short time; because she had briefly not watched what she was doing, the water was now beginning to spill over the banks. Hurriedly she unplugged the next side channel and plugged up that one; to waste water in the middle of the summer was unforgivable.

'So how is he now?'

This time she did not look up and because of the brim of her hat he could see nothing of her face. Nevertheless, he was quite certain that her expression was now one of grim and dogged determination. He watched her dam and undam two more channels as she laboured with an economy of movement and energy that came only with years of toil and he remembered how his mother had worked in exactly the same way. 'Elena, I'm not going to harm him. If that were what I intended, I'd have told the guardia to search the island and sooner or later they would find him. Then, he'd never be able to convince them of the truth. I haven't even reported the tragic death of Carlos because if that is to be done without arousing suspicion, it can only be done by Miguel when he is fit enough and can say there has been a tragedy at sea . . . What I need to do right now is to talk to him and to hear from him that he and Carlos were not running drugs.'

'No Navarro would ever touch drugs.'

'But I have to hear that from him.'

She looked along the rows to see how many more channels needed water, then said: 'Turn off.'

He walked to the edge of the field and along to the large cisterna into which the water from the well was pumped; he turned the main stop-cock to cut the flow of water. That done, he climbed on to a rock—which had been incorporated into the side of the cisterna—and stared inside; it was still half full. Lucky land to have so plentiful a supply of water. But to the people who had farmed it, it had brought only bad luck. Was that because they had not dedicated their lives solely to it, but had also gone to sea? And how stupid was he being when he wondered whether land could possibly influence the lives of men? Yet throughout the ages, men had fought because of it, so surely it had cast an influence over both their lives and deaths . . .

Elena was now walking towards the house, shoulders

bowed, pace slow and deliberate, mattock in her right hand. He knew a sudden rush of emotion and wanted to shout that her reward must lie somewhere ahead, but he kept silent because she would have been bewildered and that would have made him feel a fool. He went round the edge of the field, a longer but quicker route than walking back through the crops.

As he reached the dirt-floored patio, she said: 'You'll have some wine?' She went into the house.

He sat on one of the new patio chairs and stared out at the field. After a couple of minutes, Elena returned with a tray on which were an earthenware jug and three glasses; behind her came Ana, wearing a brightly coloured frock that did not suit her somewhat stocky figure.

'Where's Pedro?' he asked.

'He's asleep,' Ana answered.

'The last time I saw him, he was being fractious and you wondered if he was teething—is he better now?'

'It was only wind,' said Elena.

Ana's mouth tightened, but she said nothing. Elena filled the three glasses with wine and passed him one. The wine was rough. 'It's good,' he said. It was always good for a man to be reminded of some of the past.

'What do you want with us now?' Ana demanded.

He noticed how drawn was her expression and how nervous her movements. Her fears had changed, not gone. Miguel would live, but might there be a second attempt to kill him, would he be charged with smuggling and sent to jail? . . . Alvarez spoke quietly and with a sincerity that could not be mistaken. First, he explained, he needed to be certain that the brothers had not been engaged in the drug trade; once he was satisfied of that, he would do everything he could to help. So he needed to speak to Miguel and in order to do that he must know where he was hiding now.

Ana looked at Elena for a decision. Miguel was her husband, but Elena was his grandmother and there were times when it was still a relief to respect age and experience.

Elena wiped her mouth on the back of her calloused, earth-stained hand. 'You're a cousin of Dolores and she is a cousin of ours.'

He nodded. He had agreed to honour the ties of kinship. He fervently hoped that he would not learn that Miguel and Carlos had been running drugs, whereupon he would have to dishonour those ties.

'He's at Son Lluher,' she said.

Son Lluher stood in a valley which was protected by two walls of cliffs that at one point were only a hundred metres apart. Tradition had it that the Moors had determined to sack and pillage the village, but had been repulsed by fifty-one villagers who had stood shoulder-to-shoulder in the gap and, facing death with pride, had successfully fought to defend their families and homes. History showed that the Moors had never attacked the village, but the villagers sensibly preferred tradition and celebrated the glorious heroism of the fifty-one in the middle of September every year.

The village had grown in size, but not by much since there was no industry and no tourism. The few foreigners who lived in it tended to be either of an eccentric or a depraved nature. In sharp sunshine it looked charming, but in winter, when low cloud stretched from mountain to mountain, it gathered a lowering, forbidding character. There were still men and women from other parts of the island who surreptitiously crossed themselves whenever they met someone from Son Lluher.

Alvarez drove up the gently rising road and came to a halt in the small square; on the far side was the stubby church in which were kept a number of bones taken from some of the fifty-one who had fallen in battle—these were said to cure erysipelas and kidney stones. He climbed out of the car and spoke to an old man, who directed him down the second side street. When he reached the fourth house, he stepped into the entrada and called out.

Catalina Daviu, a cousin of the Navarro family, middle-aged and plump-about-to-become-fat, came through from the next room. He introduced himself as a friend of Elena's and said that she had asked him to call in and see how Miguel was getting on and Catalina accepted this without question. She led him through the next room and out to a small, enclosed patio in which grew four tangerine trees and one banana palm; on the far side was a single room.

Miguel, responding to a call, came out of the room. He recognized Alvarez immediately and said wildly: 'Why d'you let him in?'

Catalina, bewildered, stared from one to the other of them.

'Elena told me you were here,' said Alvarez.

Certain that his grandmother would have suffered the torments of the Inquisition rather than betray his whereabouts if to do so could have meant he was in any immediate danger, he became calmer. 'What d'you want?'

'To find out the truth.'

'You'd best come in.' He turned and walked back into his room, his uneasy movements showing that he was still in considerable pain.

The small room smelt dusty and, despite the fact that there had been no rain for weeks, damp. The furniture was a hotchpotch of pieces which gave the impression of having been discarded from the main house at different times as they had been replaced. In one corner, and the only new thing present, was a colour TV set.

Miguel slumped down on the bed and stretched out his right leg to ease it. Alvarez chose the stronger-looking of the easy chairs. Miguel, with a nervous gesture, ran fingers through his wavy black hair. His cheekbones were high and prominent, his nose long and beaky, his mouth full and firm, his skin a leathery deep brown—knowing he went to sea, it was easy to visualize him as a corsair. 'What d'you want to know the truth about?' he asked, attempting to speak with careless indifference.

'Smuggling.'

'Then why bother me? I've never . . .'

'Your father was the smartest smuggler working from the port and until recently I'd have said you'd inherited all his skills, but now I'm wondering.'

'I'm a fisherman and that's all. If Dad did bring a pack or two of fags ashore . . .'

'One or two thousand packs at a time. You realize you could need help if it's not to happen again?'

It was obvious that Miguel had thought hard and long about that.

'Who dislikes you and Carlos so much he put a bomb aboard your boat? And why?'

'I don't know.'

'Then think. I'm here to help you.'

'How the bleeding hell can you?'

'By finding out who planted the bomb and making certain he doesn't get a second chance. And to do that I have to know why he planted it. Were you running drugs?'

'No.'

'They pay a hundred times better than any other cargo.'

'If they paid a thousand times better, d'you think a Navarro would filthy his hands with them?'

'Your father certainly wouldn't have done.'

'Neither would we.'

'So what were you carrying?'

He was still reluctant openly to admit that he'd been engaged in smuggling, but in the end he mumbled: 'Just the usual sort of stuff.'

'No one would have wanted to murder the two of you for doing what you'd always done. So you must have cut across someone who was interested in a far more profitable line and who didn't like you horning in on his racket.'

'I said, we bloody well weren't running drugs.'

'And I accepted that. So now tell me what you were carrying or doing that paid for the new car, the new furniture, the new kitchen equipment, and enough bottles to stock a bar?'

'Just the usual.'

'I promised Elena and Ana I'd do what I could for you, but if it weren't for that I'd leave you to get blown up the next time, you being so stupid . . . Let's try once more. When you were out at sea some time before the bomb, you saw another boat which attracted your attention, didn't you?'

Miguel showed his uneasy surprise, but didn't answer.

'And it did something unusual?'

He was silent for a while, then he said slowly: 'We were watching her in case the Customs had started chartering private craft. We heard the bastards sometimes do that sort of thing to try and hide themselves.'

'This was around eleven at night and it was cloudy, so how were you keeping watch on it without radar?'

'She started showing a lot of light.'

'You've made it obvious you were keeping tabs on her before that happened.'

'Well, we'd . . . we'd one of those sights which work at night.'

'An image intensifier? Where d'you get that?'

'I don't remember.'

'I suppose the army's found itself one short . . . You were watching it, but weren't picked up by radar because you were too far away, or too low in the water, or just too cunning. What did you see?'

'A parachute!' Miguel looked at Alvarez as if expecting to be angrily disbelieved.

'And?'

'Just before it reached the sea the man released himself and splashed down; all the extra lights except one spotlight were switched off and the boat manœuvred alongside and picked him and the parachute up, then sailed on.'

'Leaving you scratching your heads?'

'It didn't make sense. I mean, someone parachuting into the sea in the middle of the night with a boat waiting to pick him up.'

'You didn't hear the plane?'

'No.'

'Then the next day you learned about the plane crash and there was no mention of the pilot being rescued and you began to wonder even more about what was going on. Did you know right away whose boat it was?'

'When she came beam on, we did.'

Like any true seaman, they could recognize every craft which regularly used the port. 'What happened when it became obvious that everyone else thought the pilot had died with the plane?'

'Carlos said that since there was something queer going on we ought to have a word with Señor Bennett.'

'What he was really saying was that it would be worth your while trying to put the bite on him even though neither of you could figure out what was really happening?'

'I said it was a stupid idea.'

'Because you were against doing anything illegal?'

'You can sneer all you bloody like . . . Look, it wasn't as if whatever the Englishman was up to was doing us any harm.'

'You're prepared to live and let live, but Carlos wasn't?'

'He's always been wild and wouldn't stop to think. He had a novia who's the nicest girl you could meet and there's money in the family, but he wouldn't settle down and marry her. Said he wasn't ready to put on a straitjacket yet.'

'And since that was his character, he decided to go ahead and talk to the señor?'

'He kept on and on that we'd a chance to make some real money.'

'If that was what he was after, why didn't he ever suggest you moved into drugs?'

'He did,' mumbled Miguel, contradicting what he had said earlier. 'I wouldn't listen.' He blushed from the shame of the admission that his brother had been prepared to blacken the name of Navarro.

His embarrassment satisfied Alvarez that this was the truth. 'He saw the English señor. Did you go with him?'

'I refused to have anything to do with it.'

'What happened?'

'The Englishman laughed at him. Told him the police wouldn't believe a mere fisherman against a man as rich and as important as him.'

'Not even when there were two of you as witnesses?'

'I've just said, I wouldn't have anything to do with it.'

'Carlos would not have told the señor that you had refused.'

'Didn't make any difference. The Englishman said he'd been recording everything and if Carlos spoke to the police, he'd be up for blackmail.'

'Hadn't Carlos thought of that danger?'

'He never thought about what could go wrong.'

'If the señor refused to pay hush money, what paid for all the new things in the house?'

'A couple of days afterwards we were mending our nets when he walked along and said he wanted a word. I cleared off. Later, Carlos said the señor had agreed to pay if we kept our mouths tight shut.'

Why the abrupt reversal of policy? wondered Alvarez. Had Bennett reconsidered the situation and decided he was in a weaker position than he'd originally judged? But if he had proof that Carlos had been trying to blackmail him, he surely could be certain that that wasn't so. As a lifelong smuggler, Carlos had a strongly developed sense of survival and therefore must have accepted that if an allegation of blackmail was corroborated by a tape-recording, he was in real trouble. No, the reason for Bennett's actions had to lie elsewhere . . . The Crown and Life Insurance Company were denying the fact that Green had died in the crash; their evidence in support of this contention was far from watertight; but while Carlos's evidence in a criminal action against Bennett for aiding and assisting an attempted fraud would have carried little weight (after proof of the attempted blackmail), his evidence in the civil action would surely have provided the clinching factor. So it was Green who had been endangered by Carlos, not Bennett; it was Green who had paid the hush money, through Bennett; and it was Green who had set the bomb which had been designed to kill both brothers, since he'd no way of knowing that Miguel did not pose a threat.

Alvarez sighed. He was now satisfied that at no time had Miguel been guilty of anything beyond time-honoured smuggling. But Carlos had been murdered and his murderer had to be arrested and tried and that could not be done without publicly exposing Miguel as a smuggler, which inevitably would result in his being arrested and charged . . .

CHAPTER 16

'There's been a telephone call for you,' said Dolores, as she set the bowl of sopas Mallorquinas on the table. Her tone had been disapproving. 'I said you were out.'

'Who was it?' Alvarez asked carelessly, more interested in savouring the smell of the sopas.

She began to serve, filling each plate with the soup that was almost a meal because of all the vegetables and bread in it. 'She was a foreigner and I couldn't understand her.'

'Did she tell you her name?'

She passed a plate to Isabel. 'She wouldn't speak clearly.'

'But she did tell you it?'

'It sounded like Sierra Collans.'

'Serena Collins . . . What on earth did she want?'

'I have no idea.'

'But you must have understood something of what she said.'

'I do not have to understand anything when a person speaks so impossibly.' She passed a plate to Juan.

Alvarez filled his glass with wine. 'I didn't expect to hear from her again, that's for sure!'

'Is she the woman who . . .' Dolores looked meaningly at Alvarez.

He presumed she was remembering the flagellation. 'That's right.'

'Then why . . .?'

'I haven't the faintest idea.'

'Is it because . . .?'

'Why don't you ever finish a sentence?' demanded Jaime.

'Because it is not a fit subject for you to listen to,' she answered.

'What? Am I an infant?'

'In matters like this, you'd better be.'

That thoroughly bewildered Jaime.

The telephone rang. 'It might be her,' said Alvarez. He stood and went through to the next room.

'Thank goodness it's you so I can communicate!' said Serena.

'I'm sorry I was out earlier on, señorita.'

'If you señorita me once more, I'll throw something at you down the telephone line. My name is Serena as you well know . . . This was going to be an apologetic call and here I am, already shouting off my head like a fishwife.' Her tone changed. 'But I still haven't reconciled myself to . . . It makes me so . . . Can you understand?'

'Only with some difficulty.'

'That's a sweet way of saying that I'm being incoherent

. . . I asked the concierge to find out your private phone number since you weren't at the police station. I'm phoning to apologize for what I said last night and for walking out on you after inviting you to coffee. Will you put my behaviour down to my being a feeble and hysterical woman?'

'But I doubt very much that you are either.'

'I think that that's a compliment. So will you have the coffee with me tonight that you should have had last night?'

'I'm afraid I'm rather busy . . .'

'A truly busy man was once defined as someone who could always find time to spare when he wanted to. How about nine o'clock at the hotel?'

'Don't you think . . .'

'Recently,' she said, her tone once more uncertain and bitter, 'I've discovered how much easier life can become if one doesn't think.' She rang off.

He returned to the dining-room, sat, and began to eat. After a while Dolores's impatience became too great to be restrained. 'Was it her?'

'Yes.'

'What did she want?'

'Only something to do with the case,' replied Alvarez vaguely.

'Are you seeing her again?'

'I have to, this evening.'

'Even when you know . . .'

Jaime looked from one to the other of them, trying to work out what this was all about.

Serena was sitting at the same table outside the hotel and she waved to him as he approached. She was, he decided, a woman whose attraction had a delayed quality, because it was not entirely physical.

'Thank you for coming.' She smiled. 'To tell the truth, when you called me "señorita" over the phone, I was certain you meant to refuse the invitation. I'm so glad I was wrong . . . Let's get hold of a waiter. You'll have a brandy as well as a coffee, but I won't.'

'I will get them . . .'

'You may order, but it's understood that I pay. I need the solace of being allowed to show my remorse. But please don't assume from that that I'm saying my remorse can be expressed in pesetas. It's much too genuine.'

'I'd never think such a thing . . .'

'Of course you wouldn't and I was only pulling your leg. Don't forget, I'm descended from the martyrs of La Verry. Let me prove part of that claim. You often have trouble in relationships because you are too generous in assessing good qualities in other people. Which must make life as a detective very difficult at times. And I'm embarrassing you because you're a very modest man, so I'll shut up on the subject . . . If I remember correctly, you smoke?' She produced the silver case from her handbag and offered it.

He flicked open his gas lighter and they lit their cigarettes. As he replaced the lighter in his pocket, a waiter came across and he ordered two coffees and one brandy.

'May I change my mind and have a brandy as well?' she asked.

He changed the order and the waiter left.

She drew on the cigarette, then fidgeted with it, rolling it gently between thumb and forefinger. 'The brandy's to give me Dutch courage.'

'I beg your pardon?'

'Something to stiffen my backbone. Why it's called Dutch courage, I don't know, since the Dutch are just as brave as anyone else . . . I must begin by apologizing once more.'

'There's really no need.'

'Yes, there is. And then I've got to explain why you're so wrong.'

He was struck afresh by the warmth in her dark brown eyes. Impossible to imagine her dressed in a whore's costume, whipping a man; could she really learn that Green had found a woman to whip him without experiencing the immediate and deep repugnance that Dolores had felt? Did she not believe, or had she forced herself to believe and yet somehow to understand and through understanding to offer forgiveness . . .?

'What are you thinking?'

Hastily, he said: 'Nothing important.'

'Is that the truth? Are you sure you weren't silently condemning me?'

'Why should I?'

'Because I was so fond of Tim and according to you he was crooked; you don't believe I should be fond of a crook. Yet I can be certain that you know as well as I that when you love someone, you love them for what they are, not for what others think they should be.'

'Are there not some faults which cannot be forgiven?'

'Can there be a fault that great? Isn't love the one force that is greater than evil? . . . You think Tim was some kind of a crook. That wouldn't have mattered to me even if it had been true. It isn't. He never intended to swindle the insurance company and the only reason that he tried to increase the amount of his policy was because of me. He wanted to make certain that if anything terrible happened to him, I'd be all right financially. I told him, he was being morbid and he said that he'd no intention of dying, but fate sometimes turned up a joker. And fate . . . and fate did turn up a joker.' She looked away and out at the bay.

He longed to believe her, but sadly she had been a shade too emotional, too eager to convince him; and had she truly believed Green dead, would she not have been far more concerned with her own grief than worrying about what he thought of the dead man?

The waiter brought the coffee and brandies.

She warmed a balloon glass in the palm of her left hand. 'You do believe me now, don't you?'

He hesitated.

'But why won't you?'

'Because of the facts.' He was aware that he had sounded harsh because of his reluctance to answer.

'The facts are that Tim crashed in the plane.' She was becoming angry.

'I have spoken to a fisherman who was out in his boat and he and his brother saw a parachute descend and the parachutist was picked up by a boat which arrived the next night at Stivas, on the Peninsula. That night, Thomas Grieves booked in at a hotel there. People often keep the same initials when they change their names. His passport was a false one. He left behind an English paperback and in this was the receipt for fuel loaded in the Flèche which Timothy Green flew from Palma airport.'

'Whose boat was it?'

'A man for whom Señor Green once worked.'

'Does he admit that he picked up Tim?'

'He denies it.'

'Then why believe the fishermen and not him? Why go on and on like this? Can't you understand what it's like for me, having you say he's alive when I know he's dead? If he were alive, he'd have been in touch with me.'

'Why have you come here?'

'Why shouldn't I? The island was the last place where he was alive. I wanted to be where he'd been, to gain a few more memories for the future. Now I realize it was a mistake; God, what a mistake!'

'Why did you go to see Señor Bennett?'

'Because . . . because he and Tim had known each other. I wanted to hear all he could tell me about Tim. I only knew him for what seems now to have been so short a time . . .' She drank the brandy quickly and it caught in her throat and she coughed.

'I've just told you that two men saw him parachute down . . .'

'And you haven't gone on to explain why you're prepared to believe such a ridiculous story.'

'I believe it because one of them has since been murdered.'

She stared at him, her expression shocked.

'A bomb was planted on their boat which was meant to kill them both, but the elder brother survived. Their murder was planned to make certain that they could never testify about what they'd seen on the night the plane crashed.'

'You're not . . . Surely to God, you're not now trying to say that Tim had anything to do with that.'

'I do not yet know who was responsible,' he replied, hoping he sounded truthful. He paused, then said: 'Where is he now?'

She shook her head.

'It's much more serious than it was. Now there's been a murder and I have to find the murderer.'

'But I tell you he couldn't have done anything like that . . . I know he couldn't.'

The first doubt; the first premonition that she had not inherited all the skills of the women of La Verry and that there was a ruthless side to Green's character which she had never identified; the first bitter acceptance of the possibility that there might be truth in the story of the flagellation?

She suddenly stood and left, walking quickly.

He added sugar to his coffee, stirred, drank. He stared out at the bay. Why could there be so much beauty out there when there was so much ugliness here?

He finished his coffee and brandy, drank her brandy, called the waiter across and paid the bill. The waiter brought him the change and then showed, by his expression, what he thought of the five-peseta tip. Did foreigners never tip less than fifty pesetas? They'd ruined everything. Alvarez was glad of the chance to find something on which he could unload a little of the anger and self-hatred he felt because he had deliberately sown the seeds of doubt in Serena's mind.

As he walked along the pavement, he heard the sounds of someone running behind him, but he thought nothing of this until his left arm was gripped to bring him to a stop.

'I'm beginning to feel like the ageing diva who can't stop giving a final farewell concert,' Serena said in a small voice.

He turned. 'I'm very sorry . . .'

'I know you don't like doing what you are, any more than I like hearing what you have to say . . . Please, Enrique, just for a little while, can we pretend that there's no past and no future, only a present?'

Several British tourists, very well wined, pushed past them, loudly complaining about the local peasants who wouldn't get out of the way.

She let go of his arm and took hold of his hand. 'Agreed?'

He nodded.

'Then let's go for a walk by the sea. When I was young —which immediately brings in the past!—I used to think that the most blissful experience was to walk barefoot on sand.'

He understood that when she'd said she wanted to banish the past, she had meant that part of it which included Green, not an earlier time when life had been so much kinder and more forgiving.

When he returned home, only Dolores was downstairs; she was crocheting. 'Has everyone but you decided on a very early night?' he asked cheerfully.

'They went to bed at the usual time. It's almost midnight.'

Her tone had been so frosty that he decided there must have been a family row. He walked over to the sideboard.

'What have you got on your shoes? . . . Do look out, you're putting whatever it is all over the floor.'

He brought out a bottle of brandy and a glass before he looked down. 'It's only sand. I went for a walk on the beach.

You know, it's very lovely down in the port at night—all the lights on the water.' He poured himself out a brandy, began to walk towards the kitchen to get some ice.

'Is it? I'm always far too busy ever to have the chance to find out.'

He added ice to his drink in the kitchen, returned to the other room. She had put her crochet work into a bag and was standing. 'I'm too tired now to clear up the mess you've made; it'll have to wait until tomorrow.'

'I'll do it.'

'When a man has to do my housework, I'll be ready for my coffin.'

He tried to nudge her into a better humour. 'Is that another bedspread you're making?'

'Isabel will need two when she marries. If she ever does.'

'Why in the world shouldn't she? She's as bright as a button already and if she has half your looks when she's grown up, the men will be running after her.'

'Perhaps. But perhaps by then she will have learned what fools men are and so will have the sense not to marry.' She left the room.

It must have been some row, he thought as he switched off the lights; Jaime was in for a chilly night. It was only when he was half way up the stairs that it occurred to him that maybe there had been no row and Dolores had been waiting up for his return—like a mother clucking over her son—and his unusually cheerful behaviour had reinforced her ridiculous and utterly wrong impression.

CHAPTER 17

Alvarez rang Guardia Civil headquarters on Monday morning and spoke to a very harassed man. 'Yes, yes, of course we're doing it, but we need time. Have you the slightest idea of the size of the task?' His accent suggested he was a Galician.

Alvarez said in a conciliatory tone: 'I know it's a fairly big job . . .'

'Fairly big! Is that how you describe having to contact every single hotel and hostal on the island to check their registrations? When God knows how many of 'em don't keep proper records. Does anyone on this island ever bother to observe the law?'

'I'm afraid we are inclined to be a little independent . . .'

'Delighted to be bloody-minded, more like. You keep shouting for full autonomy. I'd give you all you want and the further off that kept you, the better.'

'About the inquiries—have you had any luck?'

'None.'

'Have you many more places to check?'

'More than enough.'

'But at the moment it looks like a blank?'

'That's the story of this island.'

Alvarez replaced the receiver, leaned back in his chair, and stared at the quadrilateral of harsh sunlight on the floor. Assume that no Thomas Grieves was registered in any hotel or hostal, then Green had either assumed a second false name—and had all the papers to back this up—or had stayed somewhere where the law did not require his presence to be recorded, or he had managed to keep his name out of any official register. For the moment it was impossible to say which was the most likely or to judge whether he would already have left the island, satisfied he'd successfully murdered both eye-witnesses, even though there'd been no report of their deaths and the only evidence he would have to go on would be the absence of their boat from the port and of them from their home . . . Assume for the moment that he'd want more definite proof of their deaths than this. Where would be the safest place on the island to hide? He might well have judged for the second time that the answer was the most obvious, since people automatically expected a hiding-place to be hidden. Bennett's house. There was the problem of staff, of course, but it seemed they were around only during the day. And Green's presence at Ca'n Herido would explain Serena's visit, or visits, there . . .

He must, he thought, somehow find a way to persuade her that there had to be a limit even to loyalty. But how, in the face of a character as steadfast as hers? He knew both irritation that she could be so deliberately blind and warm satisfaction that this was so. Not everyone was concerned only with looking after himself. Yet one thing was certain. The longer she insisted on deceiving herself, the more heart-breaking would be the moment when it became impossible to continue to do so . . . He sighed. If only she had been able to lie a little more convincingly, he would not now be so certain she had been lying, in which case he would not be taxing his brain to find the solution to a problem for which there was no solution . . . His mind moved at a tangent. It was strange that her beauty only slowly revealed itself; but once it had, she made the moon brighter and the stars more brilliant. He remembered wondering why, after so short an acquaintance, Ware had spoken about her as he had; now he knew the answer.

Alvarez stopped the car in front of the elaborate wrought-iron gates, climbed out and pressed the red call button on the speaker box. A man's voice, abrupt in tone, said: 'Yes?'

'Is that Señor Bennett? This is Inspector Alvarez. I would like to speak with you, please.'

'Perhaps some other time. I'm extremely busy.'

'I'm sorry, señor, but the matter is important.'

There was a short silence before Bennett said: 'Very well. But you'll have to be brief.'

There was a wait before the gates opened. Was the delay Bennett's way of putting him in his place? He drove through and up the winding road, past land burned brown, to the green lawn and the colour-filled flowerbeds. Beyond the raised, circular rose-bed was a white Fiesta with the usual car-hire certificate stuck on the right-hand rear window. Was Serena here again? Then he realized that the registration number did not contain a 7 and he had noticed that that of her car did.

He walked over to the front door and pressed the bell. The door was opened by Bennett.

'Come on in, Inspector. I'm sorry to have been a little abrupt and for the delay in opening the gates, but I was on the phone, long distance, and the call was urgent as well as important.'

Alvarez tried to hide his astonishment at the apology and at the friendly way in which it had been made. He stepped into the cool hall. Bennett, dressed casually yet as unmistakably expensively as usual, indicated the open doorway into the sitting-room. 'Let's go through to the patio. And since here on the island it's officially drinking time—when isn't? —let's have a drink. I can offer most things, including a genuine pulque from Mexico.'

'A brandy, if I may.'

'Neat, on the rocks, or with soda?'

'Just with ice, thank you.'

'You carry on through while I get ice for you and champagne for myself.'

Alvarez crossed the patio, seemingly twice as hot because of the contrast with the air-conditioned house, to the table by the far end of the pool; he moved one of the chairs until he could sit in the shade of the umbrella.

A couple of minutes later, Bennett came out of the house with a tray on which were an insulated ice container and a bottle of champagne in an ice-bucket. He put the tray down on the table, then went over to the pool complex and wheeled back the mobile cocktail cabinet. He poured out a very generous brandy—Carlos I, Alvarez noted approvingly—and filled a flute with champagne. 'How does the

Mallorquin toast go?' he asked, as he raised his glass. 'To an easy life and many pesetas?'

'That is right.'

'A cynic would surely say that, given the latter, the former inevitably follows since little brown envelopes play such an important part on this island. Would you agree with that?'

'I do not understand, señor.'

'No, of course not. Very correct.'

It was difficult to make out whether Bennett was inadvertently being obnoxious while trying to be pleasant, or whether his remarks were wholly malicious. 'Señor, the last time I was here I mentioned certain facts which had been established concerning your trip to Stivas.'

'And I replied that they weren't facts, they were fiction.' He drank.

'Since then I have spoken with Miguel Navarro, the brother of Carlos.'

'Is that supposed to be of any significance?'

'You knew Carlos.'

'I don't remember meeting anyone with that name. Is he somehow connected with the plane crash?'

'He is.'

'Then I'll try once more to make something clear. You insist I sailed out to pick up Green and to take him to Stivas. That is utter nonsense. He was a business associate, not a personal friend, and therefore not someone for whom I'd be prepared to act illegally. Far from it, in fact. He was a good salesman, but there was something about his character that always made me a shade wary so that . . . Let's just say that I kept a very close watch on any business deal with which he was concerned. Because I never found the slightest thing wrong, I continued to employ him, but I made certain that socially we never became close. *De mortuis nil nisi bonum*, but there was something suspect, something weak, about him; morally he had rather a casual outlook.'

'How exactly are you using the word "morally"?'

'I'm not certain that I understand the question.'

'Are you saying that his sexual habits were unusual?'

'I was talking purely from a business point of view; in business, a man's sexual proclivities are of no account . . . There are two kinds of people who work in the City; those whose word is their bond and those whose bond becomes their word. He was one of the latter. He believed that the ends always justified the means.'

'Then you cannot have been surprised to hear from him that he was intending to fake his own death in order to defraud an insurance company?'

'Had he told me that, I would not have been surprised. He never told me.'

'Carlos and Miguel Navarro saw a man parachute into the sea, after which he was picked up by your boat. When no announcement was made of the rescue of the pilot of the missing light aircraft, Carlos realized that something funny was going on and he determined to profit by the knowledge. He came here to try and blackmail you.'

Bennett made no comment.

'But you were too smart for him and taped everything he said and then refused to pay him a single peseta. He realized he couldn't expose you and Green without also exposing himself to a charge of attempted blackmail and decided he daren't take the risk. Yet having destroyed this threat, a day or two later you sought out the brothers and offered Carlos money on condition that he kept his mouth shut. That money came from Green, not you. You had little reason to be scared by Carlos's threats, but he had every reason.'

Bennett topped up his glass. 'As I've had reason to remark before, you have a very ingenious imagination. Unfortunately, it is also absurd.' His tone changed slightly and now contained a hint of mockery. 'I did not assist Green in any attempt to defraud an insurance company for the very simple reason that that would have been criminal and although I regard some law as being as much of an ass as did Dickens, I have a developed sense of survival and so take great care to observe it.'

'As I believe, back in England you always managed to keep within it even while defrauding a large number of people?'

Bennett's anger was immediate. 'What the devil d'you mean by that?' His expression and manner had become ugly, very different from earlier on.

'I understand that before you retired your business ethics—or should I say, business morals?—were ambiguous, to say the least.'

'I did nothing illegal and I'll bloody well have you up for slander if you try to say that I did.'

'I know nothing about the English law, señor, but under Spanish law there can be no slander unless there is a third person to hear what is said.'

Bennett drained his glass, put it down on the table with such force that it might easily have shattered. 'Get this straight. Every penny I made was legal.'

'Unless or until it can be proved that you were deliberately and repeatedly rigging the market so that your clients lost money to you. Green can prove that you did. So from the beginning he has stood between you and a criminal charge which explains how he is able to blackmail you into doing what he wants . . . I think that maybe he sees as much weakness in you as you see in him?'

Bennett said with vicious anger: 'Clear out.'

Alvarez stood. 'I've one last thing to say, señor. If you help Green to hide, then you risk becoming guilty of being an accessory after the fact to murder.'

Alvarez left the patio, walked through the house, and returned to his car. He sat, opened the glove locker, searched among the litter of car papers, screwed-up aides-memoires, a torn map, toffee papers, string, and paper handkerchiefs for something to write on and with. He noted down the number of the hire car on the far side of the raised flowerbed.

Once back in the office, he dialled Traffic. He asked for the name and address of the hire company who owned the car, the registration number of which he gave them. They seemed surprised he should have rung them so late in the morning; they said they'd ring him back after lunch.

The call came through just after five as Alvarez, still a little drowsy, stared down at the papers on his desk and wondered how to work out where to start on them.

'Regarding your inquiry. The firm's name is Bon Viatge and their offices are in Calle General Larrañaga, Cala Blanca.'

'Do you know anything about them?'

'Only that they're completely incompetent when it comes to records—but that's usual.'

He thanked the other, rang off. Cala Blanca was on the south coast, roughly an hour and a half's drive away. If he went there now, not even the superior chief could blame him for not making a start on the paperwork.

It was just after seven when he drove down the gently shelving road into Cala Blanca. Like so many places, it had once been an unnamed stretch of coast with sandy beaches and crystal clear water and there had been only one large house, built in the 'twenties for a South American tin millionaire eccentric enough to like solitude. Then it had been 'discovered', named, and developed; now it was a flourishing resort with hotels, hostals, apartments, restaurants, cafés, shops, and discothèques.

The car hire firm's premises were on the front. The office was small, separated by a wooden counter from the rest of the considerable space available for storing cars; this was empty except for a blue Fiesta with a stove-in front wing. The owner, in his middle fifties, his ferrety face pitted from childhood acne, his gold teeth flashing in what passed for a smile, watched Alvarez approach.

Alvarez came to a halt in front of the counter and read a notice, in English, German, and French, which regretted that there were no cars available for hire that day. He said, as he looked up: 'Business is booming?'

'With idiots wrecking every car I own?' The owner indicated the damaged Fiesta.

'But you manage to keep your head above water?'

'What's it to you if I do?'

'You can tell me something. Cuerpo General de Policia.'

'You didn't bloody think I reckoned you a tourist, did you?'

'I don't know what you reckoned. D'you keep proper records?'

'Yeah, exactly like the government says, even though they're a pack of bloody fools who know nothing about business.'

'Isn't that like all governments?'

'I only know about ours . . . Look, I'm a busy man, so let's stop horsing around. You want to know if I'll offer you a spare-time job. All right. Any time I've a customer who wants to find a car waiting when he comes into the airport, or has left a car there which needs collecting, I'll remember you. It's only a two-hour job unless the bloody customer's forgotten to leave the keys with the gatekeeper, but I'm soft and I'll call it a three-hour one, which means a thousand pesetas.' He smiled rapaciously. 'And for your part, any time there's a spot of trouble with one of my cars, you'll help it out. Understand?'

'Perfectly. But the problem obviously is that you don't.'

'Get one thing straight. I've more of you blokes looking for hand-outs than I need and some are high enough up to take care of anyone who tries to cause trouble, so it's no bloody good thinking to screw me for more than a thousand a trip.'

'Where you're going wrong is that I'm not looking for a hand-out.'

'Then what the bleeding hell are you after?'

'Information.'

One of the two telephones rang. The owner answered the call in Mallorquin, switched to French and accepted a booking. He replaced the receiver, swivelled round in his chair until he could note the booking on a systems chart pinned to a wooden frame.

'You own the white Fiesta with this number.' Alvarez passed a slip of paper across. 'Who's the present hirer?'

'Why the interest?'

'I've seen the car around and want to know who's driving it.'

'Why?'

'You've secrets in your business and I've got 'em in mine.'

The owner looked at Alvarez with dislike. 'You know something? You sound like you come from the north.'

'I do.'

'I had a cousin from Mestara who couldn't get a job up there and so came here begging me for one. Had to sack him.'

'For honesty? Who hired that Ford.'

The owner searched through a pile of slips, swore, opened a drawer and brought out another pile, secured by a rubber band, and looked through them. 'An Englishman, name of Terence Galloway.'

T.G. again, thought Alvarez with satisfaction. Strange how even intelligent criminals so seldom learned the danger of sticking with the same initials. 'What address did he give you?'

'I don't know.'

'Why not? You're required to put it on the hiring form.'

'So?'

'So find the right book and tell me his address.'

The owner still hesitated.

'Start becoming any more difficult,' said Alvarez

pleasantly, 'and I'll begin to think it my duty to find out if you're keeping two sets of hiring and insurance forms so that when a car is returned undamaged and there's no need to claim on the insurance, you can decide whether to make the hiring official or keep the good news to yourself and pocket all the money.'

'They may do that sort of thing up north, but we don't bloody do it down here.'

'There's some who say that you lot always have been slow.'

His expression bitter—the owner prided himself on being far too smart for anyone in authority—he unlocked a drawer and brought out a book of forms in triplicate.

'I'll do the checking.'

'You're saying you can read?'

The book covered the dates from July 21st to August 12th; originally there had been a hundred and fifty top and two copy pages for each hiring; now, only a hundred and fifty copy pages remained. It was, thought Alvarez, impossible to judge whether or not this was the official book, but it was a safe bet that whichever it was, a hundred and fifty hiring and insurance fees had gone straight into the owner's pocket during the period. He looked through the copy pages. On August 3rd Terence Galloway had given his address as Hotel Llureza. 'What do you remember about him?'

'Nothing.'

'Come on, think.'

'I can think from now until tomorrow and it'll still be nothing.'

Alvarez took the passport photograph of Green from his pocket. 'Now d'you recognize him?'

The owner shrugged his shoulders. 'You don't seem to understand; I'm too busy to remember.'

'Especially the demands of the tax inspector . . . Where's the Hotel Llureza?'

'Along the front.'

'Thanks. You've been a great help.'

The owner plainly found that the most unkindest cut of all.

CHAPTER 18

The hotel was already showing signs of poor construction; rising damp had stained the walls up to two metres above the ground, old cracks had been filled in but new ones were appearing, and there were rust streaks running down from the wrought-iron railings on many of the balconies. Most builders on the island were cheerful men, as well they might be since they had a job for life—every building erected in the past twenty years was going to need very extensive repairs before the next twenty years were up.

The receptionist was young, smart, and pleasant. He checked through the entries in the register, using the unsharpened end of a pencil as a marker. He looked up. 'You can't say what day he booked in here?'

'Not for certain, but it was probably on or just before the third of this month.'

The receptionist checked again. He shook his head. 'Sorry. There's no one of that name stayed here recently.'

'Then would you go back to July 16th.' Perhaps Green had come here very soon after leaving Stivas.

A few minutes later the receptionist said: 'Still no booking.'

Alvarez thanked him, returned to the car. The fact that Galloway had given a false address to the car-hire firm was proof that he had not been a straightforward tourist; that his initials were T.G. and his car had been at Bennett's house was as near proof as he was going to get for the moment that Galloway was Green . . .

*

Alvarez arrived home late for supper, but Dolores's annoyance only surfaced when he had finished his brandy, stood, and said he had to go out.

'At this time of night?' she asked sharply.

'I won't be long.'

'I thought you specially wanted to watch that programme on the telly?'

'Work has to come before pleasure.'

'Since when? Where are you going?'

'Only to try and find out something.'

'From whom?'

'The work's very confidential . . .'

'Naturally!'

Jaime looked at them. 'What are you two on about this time?' he asked plaintively.

'That's none of your business.' She began to clear the table; her actions suggested anger, but her expression was worried. In matters of the heart, men were like children, unable to see the dangers towards which they were racing; but unlike children, once those dangers had been identified to them they blindly refused to heed them but insisted on continuing into disaster . . .

Alvarez left the house, totally unworried about whether he was approaching disaster. He would, he told himself, present all the facts calmly and unemotionally; Serena would, of course, initially try to reject the conclusion to which these facts irresistibly led, but she was too intelligent a woman not to accept them finally.

She was in the dining-room, one of only eight guests still there. She smiled as she pointed at the chair on the opposite side of the table. 'Enrique, how wonderful to see you! Especially as I've been feeling rather blue and need someone to jolly me up. So welcome, knight in shining armour.'

Was it so very stupid for a nearly middle-aged man to feel his heart beat a little faster? Did age always make ridiculous what had once been romantic?

'You're off on one of your brown studies again. What are you thinking about this time?'

'That if my horse could gallop instead of just trot, I'd have been here much sooner.'

She laughed, finished her last spoonful of ice-cream. 'Let's conform to tradition and have coffee and brandy outside. There's something you should realize. You're leading me into very bad habits. Until I met you, I only drank brandy very occasionally; now it's every day.'

They had coffee and brandy outside the hotel, then left the table, crossed the road and walked on to the beach. She took off her shoes. 'Come on, this time you do the same.'

'I'd really rather . . .'

'Now! Cast aside all those inhibitions and advance to a second childhood.'

'Serena, there's something I have to say before we do anything more.'

'And from your tone of voice, I'm not going to like listening to you. Then forget whatever it is until tomorrow. This is the land of mañana—do as the Romans do.'

'I have to speak now for your sake.'

'Dammit, why do people always become so eager about other people's sakes?'

'Because they're worried about them. I can't bear to see you get hurt any more.'

'When I learned about Tim's death I promised myself that I'd never take anything more seriously so that life could never hurt me again. But it's not all that easy to banish the past. You've discovered that, haven't you? I can see it in you . . .'

'You virtually admitted last time that you know he's alive.'

'For God's sake, don't start that again.'

He longed to stay silent, but knew that the longer he did so, the greater must be the hurt she eventually suffered. 'Let's sit down.'

She sat on the sand and he settled by her side. Still without speaking, she reached out and gripped his hand, asking for, and receiving, comfort.

'I now know almost everything,' he said sadly. 'Señor Green decided to defraud the insurance company by staging an air crash from which it must seem he could not possibly have escaped; in fact, he'd made certain Señor Bennett would pick him up at sea after he'd jumped from the plane. In the past, Señor Bennett had found a way of defrauding rich men that was safe so long as no one could prove that his intention was to defraud them; Señor Green, who'd worked for him, could provide that proof and his price for silence was Señor Bennett's help.

'As soon as the boat docked in Stivas, Señor Green went ashore; because it was too late to travel that night, he booked in at a hotel, under the name of Thomas Grieves, and the next morning he took a woman back to the hotel—'

'No!'

'I'm very, very sorry but that is what happened.'

'But he couldn't have done such a thing . . .'

And then she leant against him and he felt her shaking and he knew that she was at last accepting the bitter truth. He put his arms around her and stared out at the bay.

'I didn't know . . . I never thought . . .' Her voice died away.

He held her tighter as the words raced through his mind. She hadn't known that Green was a masochist . . . Although he'd assured himself again and again that this must have been so, one small and nasty part of his mind had repeatedly reminded him that there were women who were ready to condone, or even liked, perversions . . .

After a while, he continued speaking. 'Señor Green returned to this island either because he thought there might be trouble—and here could be one of the safest places to hide—or because by then he knew there was trouble. Señor Bennett was threatened with blackmail at the hands of a fisherman who, with his brother, had been at sea on the Saturday night. The señor refused to be blackmailed, saying he'd taped the threats, and the fisherman became too frightened to pursue the blackmail. Then, a couple of days later, Señor Bennett offered him money to stay silent. The only possible explanation for this unnecessary change of attitude is that Señor Green had told him to pay because the fisherman's evidence would, in a civil court, be fatal to the plan to defraud the insurance company.

'Blackmail is a crime that only finally ends when the victim has nothing left. Señor Green knew this and that now there was only one way of making certain he was not financially bled white. He decided to kill the brothers. He planted a bomb aboard their boat that was detonated by a trembler and timing device; the trembler was activated by the movement of the boat, which made certain they'd put to sea, and it started the timing device, which made certain they were well out from shore when the bomb exploded. But the elder brother was very lucky and was up for'd and he survived the explosion to be picked up by another boat.

'I know Señor Green is on the island because he hired a car in Cala Blanca on the 3rd and has been at Señor Bennett's in it at least once. He is a murderer, a fraudster, and a . . .' He stopped. The word 'pervert' seemed to echo. 'Serena, he's rotten through and through. I'm going to have to find and arrest him and if you're with him you'll be inculpated in the fraud and possibly even in the murder, although you had nothing to do with that. So please, please leave him.'

After a while, she said, in a low voice: 'You shouldn't have told me a lot of that, should you?'

'Perhaps not.'

'You're a policeman, yet you're warning me even though you're quite certain I helped him with the fraud. You're betraying your duty.'

'I can't help that.'

'Why not?'

'Surely to God that's obvious?'

Her answer was to brush his cheek with her lips. He began to turn his head, but she put a finger on his cheek. Conscious that her emotions must be in a state of such turmoil that the last thing she'd want would be further emotional stress, he forced himself to relax.

She spoke in a distant voice. 'I tried to tell you the other day what kind of a man he is, but I don't suppose I succeeded. He's so full of the fun of living that with him the world becomes painted in glowing colours; even walking down a road you've walked a hundred times before becomes wonderfully exciting . . . I suppose you're asking yourself how, after all my proud boasting about being descended from the women of La Verry, I failed to see what kind of a man he really is. The answer's very simple. As I once hinted, when my own emotions are involved I can be as blind as the next person—I see what my emotions want me to see and not what's actually there. But just occasionally when I was with him something would happen momentarily to lift the blindfold and I'd gain sight of something that scared me. He always knew when that had happened. He'd whirl me back into a state of blindness.'

'But surely you couldn't hide from yourself the nature of the intended fraud?'

'Of course not.'

'Didn't that tell you what he's really like?'

'There's no connection. And you know there isn't.'

'A man who's so ready to commit one crime—'

She broke in. 'Can be the nicest and kindest person you'll ever meet. You're a policeman and so have to condemn crime, but you're far too humane really to believe what you've just tried to say—that every criminal is morally rotten. Steal to feed your starving children and the law says you're a criminal; do you morally condemn the thief? Buy a company, strip it of its assets and throw out of work its previous employees, and legally you've just been clever; morally, I say you've committed a crime.'

'If everyone thought like you, there would be chaos.'

'Not chaos, because morality would reign and morality looks at all the circumstances which the law never does . . . And for me, when a man has worked for years and his work has made his employer very rich and then he is thrown aside, he is owed. So why shouldn't he claim his debt, if to do so will hurt no one?'

'You cannot defraud without hurting.'

'To a company that is worth billions, what Tim set out to get was no more than petty cash. Enrique, you're arguing because you feel you ought to, not because you believe what you're saying.'

Was she right? He didn't know. If he believed a crime like fraud branded a man as rotten, what was he since he was trying to find a way of proving Green had murdered Carlos without exposing Miguel's smuggling activities? Why, when he knew she had been an accomplice to fraud, had he warned her about Green and so betrayed his work?

'I'm feeling all cold inside; perhaps I've taken off too many layers of internal protection. Do you mind if we go back to the hotel?'

'Please remember all I've told you and don't see him again.'

She stood, waited until he was on his feet and then came forward to kiss him gently on the lips, once more breaking free before he could respond. 'If it won't embarrass you too much, I'll tell you a secret. You're a rather wonderful person.'

They left the beach and returned to the hotel and she came to a stop by the side of the first of the outside tables. 'I'm going to go straight up to my room and have an early night. Maybe the world will look brighter when I wake up.'

'May I see you tomorrow?'

'I don't know. I'd really like to, but . . . Stripping isn't ever as much fun for the stripper as for the audience.'

'I haven't enjoyed—'

'That wasn't what I was trying to say . . . Good night, sweet prince.' She stared at him for a second, her deep brown eyes filled with emotion, then turned and walked quickly into the hotel.

He returned to his car. He had had to make her understand and accept what kind of a man Green really was. But did anyone ever thank the person who stripped away one's illusions?

CHAPTER 19

Alvarez stepped into the entrada of Cristina's house and called out. Her mother came through from the room beyond and screwed up her eyes, since she should have been wearing glasses, as she stared at him. 'Enrique! I haven't seen you for a time; not since Julio Gomila's christening.'

'That was a spread and a half!'

'Had you seen the like of it before? I told Caty, when she has a christening, she can't expect anything like that. They say it cost the family over three hundred thousand pesetas. Where could they have got that sort of money?'

'I reckon it's probably better not to ask.'

She laughed, showing a wide gap in her front teeth.

'How's your back now—Cristina said it's not been too good?'

'That it hasn't and the doctors don't seem to be able to do anything about it. Just give me pills and tell me I've got to expect that sort of thing as I get older. Doesn't need a doctor to tell me that . . . But come on through and have something to drink.'

He followed her into the next room and sat in a very comfortable armchair as she poured him out a brandy.

She asked him how his family was and then told him at considerable length how hers was. Only when she'd poured him out a second drink and handed him the glass was he able to bring the conversation round to Cristina.

'You're not saying she's in trouble?'

'Good Lord, no. It's just I want a word with her.'

'You had me worried . . . She won't be back until later.'

'I expect she told you I didn't recognize her at first because she'd grown so beautiful?'

'Aye, she did. And it's that that makes me worry. With her looks, the men keep after her. I said, they'll offer all the gold in the world if only she'll open her legs to 'em, but if she does all she'll ever see will be sneers.' She was another woman who had been brought up on a farm and spoke about sexual matters in a direct manner. 'You'll have seen all the little bastards there are around the village these days and the mothers as bold as brass. When we were young, if a woman had a bastard she kept right out of sight. Times have changed.'

'That's true enough.'

'And I'm too old for all the changes.'

'Can't say I'm happy with most of them . . . So about when d'you expect Cristina back from work?'

'She never leaves the house before six and sometimes not even then because the señor tells her to do something more. When he does, there's never any more money for her. You'd think with all he's got, he'd pay her something extra.'

'He obviously wants to stay rich.' He drained his glass. 'I'll be back later on, then: and tell her it's only to ask a couple of questions about a car and to show her a photo.'

He returned just after seven, parked his car, and walked along the pavement, past a couple of gossiping women who sat out on chairs. The last time he had seen Cristina she had been wearing a navy blue and white maid's dress, notable only for its decorous utility; the colourful frock she now had on appeared to him to have but one object and that was to reveal by suggestion all that it hid. If he were young, he'd be one of the young men offering her a fortune in gold . . .

Her mother, knitting, was in the second room and she greeted him, then told Cristina to pour him out a brandy. Once again, he first spoke about family matters, observing good manners, before questioning Cristina. 'I expect your mother told you that I'd like a chat about how things are up at Ca'n Feut?'

She nodded. Her eyes were bright with curiosity.

'You told me Juana Esteva is the cook?'

'That's right.'

'Yet the first time I went up there, she opened the door.'

'When it's my day off, she has to do that sort of thing and a bit of housework as well; the señor wants things dusted every day.'

'Then you seem to have the best of the bargain since you don't have to do the cooking when it's her day off.'

Her mother said: 'She's too lazy to learn. Yet as I keep telling her, how will she ever make a good wife until she can cook.'

'Perhaps I don't want to be a good wife.'

Her mother's lips tightened. Alvarez quickly changed the subject. 'So what happened yesterday? When I went up, the señor opened the door himself. Was it your day off?'

'That's right.'

'Then Juana was ill?'

'No. The señor gave her the day off.'

'Does he often do that?'

'Well, I . . .' She looked surprised, as if she hadn't considered the question before. 'I suppose that's the first time since I've been working up there.'

'Did he give Juana any reason?'

'She's not said that he did.'

'Has he had any guests recently?'

'There was one last night.'

'Male or female?'

'I wouldn't know. They'd gone before I'd arrived and there wasn't anything said.'

'How do you know there was someone?'

'The señor said to tidy the main guest-room. I stripped the bed and vacuumed the carpet and took the towels from the bathroom for washing; all the usual.'

'Have a look at this, will you?' He passed her the photograph of Green. 'Have you ever seen him at the señor's?'

She shook her head as she returned the photograph. 'Never.'

'There was a hire-car parked outside the front door yesterday—a white Ford Fiesta. Was that there when you arrived this morning?'

'Didn't see any car.'

'Have you seen a white Fiesta up there recently?'

'Well, there's the señorita's, but no one else's.'

'That's it, then; thanks for helping.'

'So what's it all about?'

'Just something that needs checking up.' He finished his drink. 'I'd better be moving on, but before I do, will you tell me where Juana lives?'

Calle Aragón, one of the narrowest of streets in the village, was on the north-east side. Esteva was a carpenter and his workshop took up the whole of the ground floor of his house; throughout a working day the sounds of wood being sawn, planed, and hammered, echoed along the road.

Alvarez climbed the stairs to the family's accommodation, on the first and second floors, and Juana answered his call. She said she was busy preparing supper, but if he liked to talk while she got on with the work, that would be all right. They went through a room in which two young boys were watching television and into a well-equipped kitchen.

'I can't say why the señor gave me the day off,' she said,

as she stopped peeling an onion and used the back of her hand to brush the tears from her eyes. 'These things make me weep!'

'Dolores always has a good cry when she peels an onion . . . He didn't give you any sort of a reason?'

'Just phoned me to tell me not to bother to turn up. I wasn't going to argue with him!'

'Cristina says there was a guest staying last night. Have you any idea who it was?'

'None at all . . . Give me that saucepan by your elbow.'

He passed it across. She began to chop up the onion and to sweep the pieces into the saucepan.

'Have you seen a white Ford Fiesta parked up at the house recently; not the one used by the señorita.'

She shook her head as a tear trickled down each cheek.

He showed her the photograph of Green and she reluctantly stopped work long enough to look at it. 'Never seen him.'

He thanked her and was surprised that she showed no curiosity about the reasons for his questions. She said that she supposed he could find his own way out and as he left she finished chopping up the onion and reached for a couple of carrots.

Back in his car, he did not immediately start the engine and drive off, but stared blankly through the windscreen, drumming his fingers on the wheel. It seemed fairly obvious what had been the sequence of events. Green's attempt to fake his own death had run into serious trouble which could only be overcome by the deaths of the Navarro brothers. He'd thought he had executed their murders so perfectly that no one would ever suspect they'd been murdered, but then had learned that one of them had survived. So now, if it were shown that he was definitely alive, the Spanish police had a direct interest in finding him, which they had not had before. The island had ceased to be a safe hiding-place, but had become a very dangerous one from which he had to escape as soon as possible. But in the height of the season it could be very difficult to get a flight at a moment's notice and any of the ferries now running would land him in Spain, which was the last place where he wanted to be. Criminals so often panicked when the law seemed to be closing in on them; he'd decided that in the intervening time before he managed to make his escape, he must force Bennett to shelter him (prior to this he'd obviously not been staying at Ca'n Feut, as had seemed possible, although he might well have been a frequent visitor after the staff had left). Bennett, all too aware that his part in events was known, recognizing the risk but unable to persuade Green to keep as far away as possible, had done what he could to limit the dangers. Luckily it was Cristina's day off, so he had told Juana not to turn up either and in that way had made certain the staff would not see Green. But he'd made two mistakes—what criminal didn't make mistakes? He had let the hire-car remain in sight outside the house, never thinking it would arouse any interest—which, in fact, it wouldn't have done if it hadn't been seen by someone who knew it was like the car Serena had hired and had reason to wonder if, in fact, it was hers. And he had not tidied up the guest-room but had told Cristina to do that; perhaps it had been work that it was beneath his dignity to do . . .

Green must have discovered the danger he was in from Serena. Why had she told him everything she had learned? Not, Alvarez was certain, because she still loved him. She had finally accepted what kind of a man he really was and it was surely not in her character to love a weak, lying pervert. No, she had warned him because she was a woman for whom the ties of loyalty even outlasted those of love . . .

There was one way in which to check that his surmises were correct. He finally started the engine and drove home. Once there, he telephoned Motos Bon Viatge.

'What d'you want now?' demanded the owner sourly.

'Has Señor Galloway returned the car he hired?'

'Left it at the airport and someone's just gone in to collect it.'

As Alvarez replaced the receiver, the unwelcome thought occurred to him that unless he could think up some way of quietly altering one or two of the facts, he was going to have to confess to Salas that Green had been hiding at Ca'n Feut when he'd called there.

CHAPTER 20

Dolores spoke across the dining-room table to Alvarez. 'I met Elena this afternoon. She says that Miguel is nearly well enough to return home.'

There was a silence.

'Well?'

'Things aren't that easy. He can't go back yet.'

'Why not?'

'Because if he appears in public I'll have to start asking him questions and that means naming him a witness in respect of Carlos's murder. If I do that, inevitably he'll be exposed as a smuggler and there'll be nothing I can do to prevent him being in serious trouble.'

'Then you do not make him a witness.'

'But don't you understand, he's got to be if Carlos's murderer is to be caught and punished.'

She thought about that for a moment, her brow furrowed. 'It's ridiculous. Why make such a fuss about a little smuggling?'

'It's the law.'

'And you prefer the law to your own flesh and blood?'

'In fact, they are really only very distant relations of yours . . .'

'Which makes them relations of yours. But to you that

means less than nothing? You do not understand the ties of kinship?' She stood with one swift, graceful movement. 'Pass the dishes along.'

'Hey!' said Jaime hurriedly, 'I want some more.'

'You're becoming fat and are going on to a diet. You'll have nothing more to eat or drink this meal.' She carried two of the dishes through to the kitchen.

Jaime stared angrily at Alvarez. 'Look what you've done, you bloody fool.'

Alvarez was outraged by the injustice of that. He reached for the bottle of brandy.

'And you,' said Dolores from the doorway, 'have also had more than enough to drink already.'

There were times when life really was not worth living.

Rain, the first for weeks, fell during Thursday night, but it was only light and by nine on Friday morning the sky was once more cloudless; but for a while there was a hint of freshness in the air.

Alvarez looked across the office at the calendar which hung on the wall and puzzled over the date until he realized that he had still not yet torn off July. It called for too much effort to get up and put things right, so he used his fingers to work out how long it was since he had seen Serena. Several days, yet she had promised to contact him as soon as she felt emotionally stable. Perhaps she'd tried to get in touch with him either here or at home and the guard had forgotten it or Dolores had deliberately not told him because she was being totally unreasonable. He used the internal telephone to ask the guard on the front desk whether there had been a telephone message for him; there had not. He looked at the outside line, but decided it would be wiser not to ask Dolores directly, but to wait until he was at home and then to approach the matter obliquely.

He checked the time and was delighted to discover it was coffee-time. Afterwards, since he could no doubt find good reason to go down to the port, he might as well call in at the Hotel Regina and leave a message for her . . .

Three-quarters of an hour later, he spoke to the receptionist at the hotel and asked if Señorita Collins was in.

'The señorita booked out on Wednesday morning.'

'But . . . but that's impossible.'

The receptionist looked curiously at him before rechecking a list. 'It's right enough, Inspector.'

A woman, middle-aged, stout, dressed in a T-shirt and very brief shorts which might have suited a shapely eighteen-year-old, pushed past Alvarez, almost knocking him off his balance. In adenoidal, South Kensingtonian English, she demanded to know where was the car that she and her friend had ordered for eleven o'clock. The receptionist politely said he was sorry to hear it had not been delivered and would immediately ring the hire company. She didn't thank him, but angrily muttered that everyone on the island was totally incompetent before she stamped off.

Alvarez said: 'Have you any idea where she's gone?'

'No, but I know exactly where I'd like to send her.'

'I meant, Señorita Collins.'

'Oh! Hang on, will you, while I find out what's happened to the old cow's car.'

Three minutes later, the receptionist replaced the receiver. Alvarez asked him whether he'd been on duty when Señorita Collins had booked out.

'No. Francisco must have been.'

'If he's around, I'd like a word with him.'

'I'll find out if he is.'

Alvarez went over to a chair and sat, mopped his forehead, face, and neck with a handkerchief. Had he misjudged the way she would react because he had forgotten that there were women so loving and loyal that they rejected all logic and all experience; women who gained so intense a pleasure from sacrifice that they forgave even the crassest betrayal?

But could even the most forgiving of women condone a brutal murder, the motive for which was greed . . .?

Francisco, whom Alvarez had met on his first visit, came up to the chair. 'You want to know about Señorita Collins? There's nothing I can tell you, really. She asked for her account, paid it, and left.'

'You've no idea where she was off to?'

'None at all.'

'How did she leave here—by taxi?'

Francisco shook his head. 'I asked her if she wanted me to order her one, but she said someone was meeting her. She waited a few minutes and then a man turned up and she went off with him.'

'Have you any idea who he was?'

'Never seen him before.'

'English?'

He shrugged his shoulders.

'Can you describe him?'

'I was being driven crazy by a party of guests who wanted to book an excursion, but couldn't decide which to choose and kept on and on asking stupid questions. I saw him with her and that's all.'

'Try and remember something about him. Was he tall, clean-shaven, and with a long, narrow face that had an expression on it which suggested he thought everyone else needed a bath?'

'It's no good. He was dressed casual, but still looked smart; that's all I noticed.'

Alvarez left the hotel and walked slowly along the front road towards his parked car. That the man had been smartly dressed was hardly a definite description, yet he was certain the man had been Bennett. Come to collect Serena to take her to Green? But the car hired by Green from Motos Bon Viatge had been left at the airport, suggesting he'd flown from the island. A bluff on top of a bluff? Had he decided to remain because it was so obvious that he must flee once the original bluff had been exposed? If so, then despite all she'd said, Serena had forsworn her resolve to have nothing more to do with him . . .

He had to discover where she'd gone and somehow find the words that would finally strip away the last illusion and force her to understand that there were times when love and loyalty ceased to be admirable traits and instead became stupid and deadly dangerous.

CHAPTER 21

As he stepped into the entrada of Folchs' house, Alvarez felt the tension mount until it seemed to be squeezing his breath. Would either Cristina or Juana be able to tell him what he must know?

Cristina came into the room. 'I thought I recognized the voice. It's strange, isn't it? You don't see somebody for years and then you see 'em every other day.'

There was a hint of excitement in her manner which made him think that she would soon be meeting a boyfriend. If he had the powers of a fairy godmother, he'd wish her the most valuable of all gifts—that she be allowed to escape the more bitter complications of personal relationships.

'Here, are you all right?' she asked, with sudden concern.

'Just thinking . . . You'll remember that photo I showed you?'

'Sure.'

'Has the man turned up at Ca'n Feut in the past couple of days?'

'I haven't see him.'

'Could he be in the house without you knowing—are there rooms you don't normally go into?'

'No way. The señor's crazy about keeping the place clean

and tidy and I have to dust in every single room most days.'

'You know Señorita Collins, don't you?'

'That's right.'

'Have you seen her recently?'

'She's been around for the past couple of days.'

'When was she last up there?'

She said, in puzzled tones: 'I'm saying, she's staying there.'

'Are you sure?'

'Couldn't be surer.'

He spoke aloud, but more to himself than to her. 'But if Green isn't there, she's on her own and . . .'

'I wouldn't say it was like that.'

'Why not?'

'Don't you understand?'

And suddenly he realized what she was inferring. 'How dare you!' he said violently.

She stepped back, momentarily frightened by his sudden anger.

'Keep your vile ideas to yourself.'

Her fear, since she had considerable spirit, turned into resentment. 'Why are you shouting at me like that?'

'It's disgusting to suggest she'd have anything to do with the señor.'

'Hasn't anyone told you, that sort of thing happens these days.'

'I know what goes on better than you do and I also know that there are still some people who are decent.'

'You sound like my Aunt María . . . I make the beds, right? And I've only been making the one in his room because none of the others has been used even though she's staying there. And I'll tell you something more. From the look of the sheets in the morning, the bed's not been used just for sleeping.'

He longed to believe that she was merely gaining a salacious excitement from lying, but he could not deny his conviction that she was telling the truth. An aching, despairing sadness began to freeze his mind.

She stared at him. 'Something is the matter! Are you feeling rotten all of a sudden? Can I get you a drink?'

He shook his head, turned, and crossed to the front door, only vaguely aware that she was saying something more. He left the house and walked along the pavement, with the shuffling steps of someone old, passing a man who was beating out the wool from a mattress. How could she? Bennett was immensely wealthy whereas Green, if his attempt to defraud the company failed, had little to offer. But knowing her, it was impossible to accept so facile and sordid an explanation. So what could make her give herself to Bennett on so short an acquaintance? Slowly and painfully he began to understand. When a woman of her nature discovered she had been deceived and betrayed by the man she loved, her sense of loss was far more acute than it would be for another, and less emotional woman; so acute, in fact, that love became hate and loyalty disloyalty, since one was the mirror image of the other. How best could she express her newborn hate and disloyalty? By giving herself to a man she disliked because this was the opposite of the reason for which she had previously given herself . . .

But understanding did not ease the ever-growing pain. On the contrary, it increased it because he could judge how she would be hating herself even as she revenged herself.

He was only a few hundred metres from the entrance gates of Ca'n Feut when a yellow Porsche rounded the corner in front of him and passed at a speed which rocked his car. The Porsche had been going too fast for him to identify the driver, although he could be certain there had been no passenger, but it was the kind of car he would have expected Bennett to own. If it had been Bennett's, and Serena was up at the house, he'd the chance to speak to her on her own.

He reached the gates, spoke to Cristina over the speaker,

then drove through and up the winding road. Cristina opened the front door.

'Is the señor in?' he asked.

She shook her head. 'He left a moment ago to collect the mail . . . Are you better today?'

'Yes, thank you . . . And the señorita?'

She looked curiously at him, intrigued by the tone of his voice. 'She's out by the pool.'

Serena, lying on a chaise-longue, was wearing a brief bikini and despite the fact that her figure was fuller than would normally have been advisable in so skimpy a garment, she was flattered rather than mocked. She turned her head and watched him approach, her eyes hidden by reflective dark glasses.

He'd thought of many opening sentences, any one of which would have subtly reminded her how hurt he must be, but as he came up to her, he blurted out: 'You've never called me.'

'I said I'd be in touch when I felt ready.' There was neither warmth nor any suggestion of remorse in her voice.

'But . . .' He stopped.

'Why have you come here?'

He had expected embarrassment, hoped for contrition, found only rejection. Bewildered, he gestured with his hands. 'But surely . . .'

She came to her feet. 'You'd better come inside and have a drink.'

As his bewilderment slowly became replaced by bitterness, he followed her around the pool and into the house. The mobile cocktail cabinet was near a display cabinet and she gestured at it. 'Pour yourself out what you want. I'm going to put on something; Pat keeps the air-conditioning so high the house is like an ice-box.'

He watched her walk the length of the room to pass through the doorway and the smooth movements of her flesh filled his mind. Cursing his weakness—please God he would soon reach an age when the desires of the flesh were lost—he crossed to the cocktail cabinet, opened the two top flaps which brought up the shelf of bottles, and poured himself a very large brandy.

When she returned, she was wearing a pink towelling robe. 'Have you found what you want?'

'Yes, thanks. What can I pour you?'

'A red vermouth with soda and lots of ice.'

'There isn't any ice.' The formal politeness with which they spoke mocked him.

'I'll go and get some.' She left, to return with an insulated ice-bucket which she handed to him. Their fingers briefly met and the touch was, for him, painful. He poured out a vermouth, added soda and ice, carried the glass over to the large settee where she now sat. He returned to the cocktail cabinet and dropped three ice cubes into his brandy, went over to an armchair. 'I'm sorry if I sounded . . .'

She interrupted him. 'Enrique, let's be completely straight with each other. I'm sorry if you feel I've done something wrong, but although we had good fun together, it was never more than that.'

'You know it was.'

'Not as far as I'm concerned.'

She'd spoken with such cold conviction that he momentarily found himself wondering if he had been totally and ludicrously mistaken about her.

'So that's why I didn't get in touch with you again. There was simply no point in it.'

He said slowly: 'Something's happened, hasn't it?'

'Lots of things have happened.'

'But something which has completely changed you. Why are you staying here?'

'Obviously, because I want to.'

'But how can you want to?'

'You can't understand? You should, since you're responsible.'

'Me?'

'You went on and on until you convinced me of the kind of man Tim really is; it's you who destroyed my illusions.'

'I had to. You couldn't go on believing a lie. But why let that make you come here?'

'Why not?'

'The truth is, isn't it, you're here because you discovered you'd been so terribly betrayed? You're trying to get your own back on Señor Green by humiliating yourself. For God's sake, stop it. What you're doing now can only make you hate yourself later on . . .'

'God Almighty, you're old-fashioned enough to be able to remember the dinosaurs! You do know Queen Victoria's dead, don't you?'

'Why are you acting like this?'

'Because you're talking like a blind fool. Do you really think in the world of today there's still room for verray parfit gentil knights and ladies fair whose lives are governed by the laws of the courts of love?'

'There is still room, yes.'

'Then like the dinosaurs, you're not going to survive . . . I'll tell you exactly why I've moved in with Pat. There's nothing romantic about the reason. I'm not nearly complicated enough to set out to humiliate myself in order to gain revenge. That strikes me as being just plain bloody silly since it means suffering twice over. I'm here because I've no money and if Tim tried to give me some, I wouldn't touch a penny of it even though I'd do almost anything rather than be poor. You talk about humiliation; there's no humiliation more terrible than poverty. Pat's rich. If you'd been rich, I might have been in touch with you again; but you aren't.'

She drank and as she did so the loosely tied towelling robe fell open and ironically the picture she now presented was far more erotic than when she had been coatless. Desire, fuelled by bitterness and despair, flamed in his mind. He stood, crossed to the settee, ran his hand under her bikini top to cup her left breast as he kissed her wildly.

She struggled to free herself, then swung her left hand round to hit him on the side of his head. The blow brought him back to his senses. He jerked his hand free and stepped back.

'You'd better go.'

He gestured with his hands, pleading for understanding and forgiveness. 'Now,' she shouted wildly.

Half a kilometre from Ca'n Feut the Porsche passed him, again travelling in the opposite direction, and this time he identified Bennett. The cynics were right and he was wrong, he thought; money could buy anything and especially a woman's honour.

The soup had been almost tasteless and Jaime had looked with surprise at Dolores, but in the end he had decided to observe discretion and remain silent. However, when he began to chew his first mouthful of meat and found it to be almost inedible, he could no longer remain silent. 'What the hell's happening? The soup was bloody awful and this is worse.'

Isabel and Juan stared wide-eyed at him; Alvarez continued to eat, as if totally unconscious both of the quality of the cooking and of Jaime's reckless audacity in so forcefully criticizing it.

Surprised, and heartened, by Dolores's silence, Jaime continued: 'The meat's tougher than old boots.'

'Is it?' she said disinterestedly.

'Try it.'

'I'm not hungry. And how can I worry about what kind of meat the butcher is trying to sell me when all I can think of is poor Miguel, who longs to return home to be with his family, but cannot because Enrique will not permit that.'

They looked at Alvarez. He continued chewing.

She continued, in tones of high tragedy: 'That any relative

of mine should not care enough to help a relative of his!'

Alvarez finally swallowed. 'I'm doing all I can,' he muttered.

'Are you? When Ana does not have her man or Elena her grandson? Knowing that, how can I worry about cooking?'

Jaime, his tone shocked, said: 'You're not suggesting we're going to have to eat like this until Miguel's back home?'

Her silence was her answer.

CHAPTER 22

Alvarez stared through the window of the office and, despite the fact that the sun shone as fiercely as ever, saw only grey. The phone rang. After a while, he lifted the receiver.

'Enrique, thank goodness I've managed to get hold of you. Your cousin wouldn't understand me and I was scared I'd never find you in time.'

He gripped the receiver so tightly that his knuckles whitened. 'What's happened, Serena?'

'I'm leaving soon and I must see you before I go. You will meet me, won't you? Please, it's so important.'

'Where?'

'My plane leaves at four-thirty and I have to book in by three which means leaving here by two. So anywhere you like before then.'

'How are you getting to the airport?'

'I'm ordering a taxi.'

'I'll take you. And we could have lunch in Palma first if we went soon.'

'Oh God, Enrique, life would have been so much easier if you weren't so wonderful.'

The world was no longer grey. 'Where are you now?'

'At the house. Pat's away for the morning.'

'Then I'll come up right away.'

He said goodbye and replaced the receiver, closed the shutters, and left. His car was in the square and he had forgotten to set the parking dial to the time of his arrival and one of the municipal police had made out a ticket and stuck it under the windscreen wiper; he pulled this free, screwed it up, and threw it into a nearby litter-bin. He drove out of the square and through the village faster than he normally did and once on the main road he floored the accelerator, careless of how much he was stressing the tired engine. He had to express his feeling somehow.

The gates of Ca'n Feut were open and he drove up the road to the turning circle. As he climbed out, Serena came through the doorway of the house. For him, the sight of her was like looking at a painting he knew and loved, yet had not seen for some time; he discovered fresh beauty in the natural curls of her hair, the shell shape of her ears, the high cheekbones, the cheerful nose, the sensuous mouth, the graceful neck, the shapely body; and finally in the warmth that was in her dark brown eyes.

She said in a low voice: 'I'll never be able to thank you enough for coming here.'

'There's no need.'

She briefly laid her cheek against his. 'Yes, there is.' She stepped back. 'I'll just get my suitcases . . .'

'Where are they?'

'In the hall.'

She followed him inside. 'I must find Juana to say goodbye and to give her a note from Pat. I won't be a second.'

He carried out the suitcases and put them in the car, then waited, standing within the shade of the house. When she returned, he went ahead of her and opened the passenger door; she did not make any immediate effort to climb inside, but stood, staring out at the surrounding countryside to the north and the mountains which backed this. '"Where every prospect pleases, And only man is vile." The good bishop should have been charitable enough to write some men, even though it wouldn't scan.' She finally stepped into the car and sat.

She was silent until they had left the grounds and were half way to the main road and then she rested one arm along the back of his seat and turned until she could look at him. 'You know why I was so foul to you, don't you?'

'I think so.'

'It's funny. How ever many times have I boasted to you about understanding other people, yet you understand me so much better than I do myself.'

'You told me that if your emotions became involved, you could no longer see clearly.'

'Did I? I don't remember. But it's true . . . I persuaded myself that it was because I was certain Pat could make me happy again that I joined up with him. And this when all the time I had to know, deep down, that what I was really wanting to do was to hurt Tim because he'd betrayed me and to hurt you because you'd forced me to acknowledge his betrayal; and perhaps also to hurt myself . . . You were so right—yet again. Perhaps some ancestor of yours was born in La Verry. Will you forgive me for the beast I've been?'

'I've forgotten.'

She stroked his neck. 'Why are you so wonderfully understanding?'

He showed his warrant card to the guard at the entrance of the departure area and went through. He waited whilst Serena's handbag and holdall passed through the X-ray machine, and she went through the metal detector, and then they crossed to the bar. 'We have a saying on the island . . .' he began.

'For every occasion, it seems.'

He smiled. 'We say that a last long copita makes for a short separation.'

'A saying obviously encouraged by the brandy barons.'

'Nevertheless, let's each drink a copita.'

'The longer the better?'

Before drinking, they linked their arms. 'To a very short separation,' she said. Her eyes were only inches from his and he felt engulfed by their warmth. For several seconds she remained motionless, then she sipped her drink, after which she disengaged her arm.

He offered her a cigarette, flicked open his lighter. 'How long will you be in Changres?'

'Probably until the lease runs out, which is only about another three weeks. Tim will never turn up there because that would be far too dangerous for him . . . Oh God, do we have to talk about him even now?'

'I'm sorry.'

'It wasn't your fault and you know perfectly well it wasn't . . . Shall I look into your soul just once more? You accept blame so quickly because you want to save distress. Right?'

'Perhaps. But only when I care about someone.'

She touched his arm briefly. 'Remember my jeering at you because you insisted there was still room in our lousy world for a verray parfit gentil knight? You keep proving you're right.'

He drank, wishing that time could stand still. 'What will you do after the lease is up?'

'I don't know exactly.'

'But you will tell me what is happening; and when everything is settled, we'll see each other again?'

'Do you really have to ask?'

'No. But I like to hear the answer. If you ever need any help . . .'

'My knight in shining armour will come riding?'

'Galloping.'

'In fact, do you ride?'

'No. But I will learn.'

The speakers announced that boarding would begin on Flight PF 363, destination Paris. She finished her drink. 'I hate prolonged goodbyes, so please don't wait around until I actually board; leave now.' She waited until he was standing, then kissed him. 'Au revoir, Don Quixote.' She picked up her holdall and hurried away.

Salas telephoned Alvarez on Monday. 'I've been expecting to hear from you for several days.'

'Señor, I intended . . .'

'They say the road to hell is paved with good intentions; no doubt you can confirm that fact. Have you discovered where the Englishman is hiding?'

'Not exactly.'

'What does that mean?'

'Actually, it's all a bit complicated . . .'

'Naturally.'

'The thing is . . . Well, I'm positive he's no longer on the island.'

'Why are you so certain?'

'He flew off on Tuesday.'

'That's interesting in view of the fact that I've just had a report that the inquiries among the hotels and hostals for Terence Galloway have finally been completed, without success. Is it just possible that you forgot to inform the department concerned on Tuesday that their inquiries had become unnecessary?'

Alvarez leaned over until he could slide out the bottom right-hand drawer of his desk. He was going to need fortification.

Dolores plied the crochet hook with dextrous speed; the ball of cotton thread jumped as if it had been patted. 'I saw Elena again today.'

Jaime looked at Alvarez, who concentrated even more closely on the television.

'She wants to know if it's all right now for Miguel to return home?'

Alvarez cleared his throat. 'Not really.'

'Why not?'

'I've told you, over and over again. If he appears on his own, having been injured, without his boat, it's obvious Carlos has disappeared. I'd have to ask what's happened and that would immediately make Miguel a witness; he'd have to say his brother was murdered and there'll be an investigation and he'll have to admit that he's a smuggler.'

'Everybody knows he is; the Navarros have always been smugglers.'

'The forasteros don't know that,' he said, using the term which indicated men from the Peninsula; men who would not understand the customs of an island race.

'The family has almost no money coming in. Ana needs her man, Pedro needs his father, and Elena needs her grandson.'

'Yes, of course, but . . .'

'So what are you doing about it?'

'What I can. But can't you see that the problem's really beyond me because the crime's so serious . . .'

She put down her crocheting on the small olive table, stood. Her tone was icy. 'That I should ever have to hear my cousin say that the problems of his own flesh and blood are no concern of his!'

'Why won't you try to understand . . .'

'Understand a blasphemy? . . . Now, I suppose I must go and prepare supper, since even a man who denies his own family expects a woman to feed him. But I am worn out with worry, so I can't prepare much.' She swept out of the room with the majestic grace of a prima donna who was upstaging the baritone.

'Why don't you do something?' demanded Jaime.

'What, for instance?' replied Alvarez.

'How should I know? But do you want to have to go on eating meals that aren't fit for a bloody dog?'

Cristina drove round the side of Ca'n Feut and parked beyond the double garage; Bennett did not like the staff cars to be in evidence. She let herself into the utility room, in which were the second and larger deep freeze, the washing-machine, and overhead lines for drying the washing in wet weather, and went through to the kitchen; one of her more ambitious daydreams was one day to own a kitchen as well equipped as this. To one side was a small room and she went into this and changed into her maid's frock. She checked her image in the long, upright mirror, smoothed down a curl of hair, returned to the kitchen. It had been her day off yesterday and was Juana's today and any message concerning her work would be on the pad by the food mixer, written in Juana's laboured handwriting. The top page of the pad was bare. So it was just the usual routine—thoroughly clean the master bedroom and change the sheets since they had been used for two nights (she'd never heard of another man so pernickety about cleanliness), vacuum the sitting-room, dust as many of the other rooms as possible, sweep down the pool patio, check for dirty glasses in the cocktail cabinet . . .

At midday she went out to the patio and spoke to Bennett who was swimming in the pool, cutting through the water with an elegant crawl. He had learned no Spanish and so she had to use her school English when he came to a stop in the shallow end. 'What you wish to lunch, señor?'

'Whatever there is.'

'How is that?'

'Cook whatever comes out of the deep freeze first.'

After some reflection, she was satisfied she understood. 'And you wish some vegetables?'

'Potatoes and beans.'

She returned to the kitchen where she peeled three

potatoes and cut them into small cubes, then put them into a saucepan, ready for boiling. From the refrigerator she collected a bag of French beans and took out of this a handful, which she topped and tailed. As she worked, she wondered if Juan from Cala Roig would ask her to the wine festival at Santa Eulalia when the harvest was celebrated with dancing in the street, free wine, and one of the best fireworks' displays on the island. Juan was tall, dark, and handsome. What a pity he was only a mechanic and would never be able to give her a dream kitchen . . . She finished the beans, went through to the utility room where she opened up the large deep freeze and from the end tray took out one of the meals prepared by Juana which she would heat in the microwave oven.

It was six. Cristina changed out of her maid's dress, primped her hair, and then went in search of the señor to say that she was leaving. He was in the sitting-room, watching a video tape. 'Good night, señor.'

He nodded, but did not bother to look at her.

She noticed that his expression was drawn and beneath the tan his complexion held a greyish tinge; with a quick concern which came naturally, and this despite the fact that he'd always treated her with such indifference it was as if he thought it demeaning even to be polite, she asked him if he were feeling all right?

'Yes.'

'But you no look good.'

He ignored her comment.

She shrugged her shoulders, turned and left.

The following morning, Cristina and Juana by chance arrived together at the gateway; Juana used her remote control unit to open the gates and they drove up the hill and round the house to park their cars by the side of the garage. Despite their difference in ages, they were very friendly and they chatted volubly as they crossed to the door of the utility room. Cristina turned the handle and pushed, but the door remained firm. 'It's locked,' she said with surprise.

'The señor's overslept; or maybe he's been too busy to worry about unlocking.'

They both giggled. Juana searched her purse for the key —they'd both been given one, but normally never had to use it because Bennett was a man of routine who rose early and unlocked the house.

Once in the kitchen, Juana looked at the table. 'He's not eaten the salad you put out for him for supper.'

'Nor has he! And come to that, there's no dirty crockery to put in the machine. He must have gone out . . . Only he always says if he's going to so that we don't prepare something that's wasted.'

'A man with his fortune, worrying about a little lettuce wasted!'

Cristina remembered something. 'When I left last night, I thought he was looking ill. Maybe . . .'

'You'd better go and find out.'

'You'll have to come with me.'

They first went into the sitting-room. An opened newspaper had been left on one of the chairs, there was a dirty glass on a coffee table, and the TV and video sets had been switched off by remote control, but not at the sets. A small pool of vomit was by the chair in which Bennett normally sat.

'Sweet Mary,' whispered Juana.

Apprehensively, they looked at each other.

'He must have called a doctor . . .' Cristina became silent.

They went up the stairs and along the corridor to the door of the master bedroom. Juana knocked and when there was no answer, she knocked again. Eventually, she said: 'We'd best find out if . . .' She hesitated for several more seconds before she finally opened the door. To their horror, they saw that Bennett had collapsed and fallen to the floor beyond the foot of the bed and there could be little doubt that he was dead.

CHAPTER 23

Rossello had the bouncy aggressiveness of so many small men and he was unusually pompous, but he was also a very competent and dedicated doctor. He fingered his pencil moustache as he stared down at the body on the floor. 'It would almost certainly seem to be something he ate or drank, but this naturally can only be confirmed after the post-mortem and all necessary forensic tests have been completed.'

'Can you guess what that something might have been?' asked Alvarez.

'I am in the habit of diagnosing, not guessing.'

'What I really meant was . . .'

Rossello was clearly uninterested.

Ten minutes later, after he'd phoned the Institute of Forensic Anatomy and the doctor had left, Alvarez returned to the bedroom. As he stood near the body, he shivered, not from the coolness of the air-conditioning, but because of the knowledge that Bennett had possessed so much that the world had to offer, yet his end had been lonely and frightening; not all his wealth had been unable to buy him a kind death. Perhaps this was the only consolation that the poor of the world were ever likely to receive.

The assistant professor from the Institute of Forensic Anatomy was a large, jovial man with a macabre sense of humour that sometimes shocked Alvarez, whose sense of decorum was always sharply narrowed by death.

'That's that, then,' said the assistant professor, as he

fitted the last of the plastic pots containing samples into a small leather case. 'It's OK to move him when you're ready.'

'Is there anything you can tell me now?'

'Not really. You'll have to wait until all the tests have been completed for any hard information.'

'But the cause of death was something he ate or drank?'

'There's no real doubt on that score.'

'If it was food, could it have been tainted naturally?'

'You're thinking along the lines of acute salmonella? I'd say that things happened too quickly. The maid says he was perfectly all right at midday, but looked a bit rotten at six in the evening. He was sick downstairs, but presumably didn't feel bad enough to call out a doctor or, alternately, was too muddled mentally to think of doing so. He came upstairs and then collapsed. The best estimate for time of death suggests two or three in the morning, so from being OK to death is about fourteen or fifteen hours. That calls for something fairly violent.'

'Then you're saying he was poisoned?'

'That's what it looks like right now, but I'm not saying that that is definitely the case; only the tests can do that. Do you know if anyone wanted him out of the way?'

Alvarez answered slowly: 'There is someone who could never feel safe all the time he was alive.'

Salas's secretary answered Alvarez's call and in her plum-in-the-mouth voice informed him that the superior chief was not in the office, but if the matter was urgent—really urgent—he could be contacted at the hotel where a reception was being held for senior members of the forces of law and order.

He telephoned the hotel. He spoke to three men in turn before it was agreed to call the superior chief to the phone.

'Yes?' said Salas.

'Inspector Alvarez, señor.'

'Now there's a coincidence!' The tone of voice had been jovial.

At first bewildered, Alvarez suddenly realized that Salas had probably been enjoying the hospitality and that even he must mellow after several drinks. 'Señor, I have to report . . .'

'The Governor-General is a man with a great sense of humour and when I told him about some of your cases he laughed more than I've seen anyone do for a long time. He particularly appreciated my description of you as a man who, if placed in the government, would reduce the whole country to a complete shambles even more quickly than the socialists are doing. Do you like that?'

'Yes, señor . . . Señor Bennett died early this morning. Although there can be no certainty until all the tests have been completed, it seems likely he was poisoned. This must mean that Green has not, after all, left the island.'

'Are you telling me that you have changed your mind yet again?'

'It is not really that I have changed it, señor; more, the facts . . .'

'You inform me that this Englishman, Green, is dead, after which you inform me that he is alive; you say he is in Stivas; no, in France; no, here, on the island; then that you are mistaken, he is not here, he is somewhere else; again, he is not there, he is here; no, he is not here, he is there; but he is not there, he is here . . .'

'I don't think it's really been quite that often . . .'

'The Governor-General will be even more amused when I tell him about this!' Salas was still chuckling as he cut the connection.

By next morning, Alvarez thought miserably, Salas was not going to find the matter quite so amusing.

In the sitting-room of Ca'n Feut, Cristina stared wide-eyed at Alvarez. 'Mother of God!'

'There can't be any certainty yet, but there's little room for doubt.'

'But he had his lunch here . . .' For the first time, she realized a possible implication in what had been said. 'You think I poisoned him?' Her fear became almost hysterical. 'I didn't. I wouldn't. I couldn't . . .'

He said sharply: 'I'm not suggesting anything of the sort.'

'But I cooked his lunch. I gave it to him . . .'

'And did you add poison to it?'

'No,' she shouted wildly.

'Then you didn't poison him. Just sit down, calm down, and tell me what happened here yesterday.'

At first haltingly, then with greater fluency, she described the previous day.

'Let's see if I've got this correctly. He went out at ten o'clock, you don't know where but expect it was to collect the post, and returned at roughly half eleven. He went swimming and was in the pool when you asked him what he wanted for lunch. He said he didn't mind, or words to that effect. You cooked him pork chops in a mushroom sauce, boiled potatoes, and beans. Afterwards, he had ice-cream. And as far as you can judge, he felt perfectly all right at this stage?'

'Well, he ate everything.'

'How did you make the mushroom sauce?'

'I didn't actually do anything but put the dish in the microwave oven.'

'How's that?'

'Well, like I said to you—and Mum went on about it when you were at home—I don't go for cooking, so Juana does it all.'

'Then since it was her day off, presumably she'd prepared the food beforehand and left it for you to heat up?'

'That's right.'

'But then why did you ask the señor what he wanted to eat? There wasn't really any choice for him, was there?'

'No, it's not quite like that. Juana makes half a dozen dishes at the same time and so he could have had pork chops in garlic sauce, kidneys in sherry, duck in orange, or chicken which she does with peppers, almonds, and herbs.'

'If that lot was in the refrigerator for any length of time . . .'

'Not the refrigerator, the deep freeze.'

He silently called himself a fool. A deep freeze. Which had made things so easy for Green when he'd been staying at the house. All he'd had to do was to take out one dish and defrost it until he could add the poison, then return it; that dish had become a time-bomb, exploded by the innocent party who cooked it in the microwave and served it.

And Salas would have to be told that although Green had murdered Bennett, he was not after all on the island when the murder was committed, but hundreds of miles away . . .

The weather usually broke towards the end of August and this year was no exception. The sky clouded over during the early part of the night and by daylight the rain was steady. Tourists complained bitterly, farmers rejoiced and stared out at their crops which would not need irrigating for at least a couple of days.

Alvarez sat behind his desk and tried to find a reason for not starting on the mountain of paperwork. After a while he sighed and reached for the top sheet of paper on the nearest pile. It proved to be a memorandum headed Urgent, from Salas's office, dated two and a half weeks earlier . . . The telephone rang and he dropped the sheet on to the desk.

'Inspector Alvarez? I have a call for you from Professor Ochivera.'

There was a brief pause before Ochivera said: 'The post-mortem has been concluded and the cause of death is confirmed as poisoning. While you will have to await the findings of my colleague, Professor Fortunato, for the nature of the poison positively to be identified, you may accept that the active principles were amanitine and phalloidine; there was the typical inflammation around the eyes and of the mucous membranes of the gastric and intestinal tracts. Perhaps the commonest source of those two principles is *amanita phalloides*, better known as the Death Cap. Part of one will lead to serious illness, two mean certain death.'

'You're talking about the mushroom?'

'The fungus,' corrected Ochivera.

'Wasn't there a case on the island many years ago . . .' Alvarez tried to pin down the memory.

'You are probably thinking of the late eighteen-nineties when several people died in a village in the Sierra de Torrelles. The science of toxicology was not advanced then and it was some time before the Death Cap was suspected; especially since experts had previously held that the fungus did not grow on the island. Subsequently, it has been found in several locations, always near oak and at a height of between one and three hundred metres. The deadly peril of the Death Cap is that it is easily confused with edible fungi, especially the field mushroom, and it is neutral in taste or even slightly pleasant.'

The pork chops had been in a mushroom sauce so it had been simple for Green to find a pack which perfectly suited his murderous plans . . .

'There is one last point of interest, although it has not, in fact, any direct connection with the poisoning. The buttocks of the dead man bore several abrasions. It is impossible to speak with any certainty, since the marks were caused many days ago and are now faint, but it's my opinion they were caused by a whip. An investigation into the dead man's character would probably show that he was of a masochistic persuasion.

'That's all. You will, of course, receive a written report in due course; and my comments concerning the source of the poison must be treated as provisional until you hear from my colleague.'

Alvarez mumbled a goodbye, replaced the receiver. Blankly, he stared out through the window, trying, but failing, to cut short his questioning mind. Green had been a masochist. Now it appeared that Bennett had also been one. Was that a coincidence, or the key to what had really happened? With a growing, sick despair, he knew that the answer was the latter . . .

He would, of course, have understood the truth much earlier, and saved himself untold bitter sadness, if only he'd had the wit to realize that this case had been as much about characters as facts. During the course of their friendship, Serena had revealed to him her own and Green's characters, but because he was not clever and his emotions had become involved and because he had already formed his judgements, and had not listened carefully enough to appreciate the significance of all she'd said . . . Or to understand that when someone had so clearly acted out of character—could she really have fallen in love with a weak, perverted man who'd betray her at the first opportunity?—there had to be a reason, which must be that the facts as presented were wrong . . .

Green. A fast talker, a superb salesman, enjoying life to the full; married to a woman who was only comfortable in a suburban sitting-room and forever worrying about what the Joneses thought; seeking an emotional relationship, the depths of which were quite beyond his wife's ability—or wish—to provide; possessed of a strict sense of morality which, however, owed nothing to conventional thought or the dictates of the law . . .

Bennett. Sharp, clever, hard-headed, and so selfish that he was unable accurately to assess the qualities of others; ruthless where his own interests were concerned; indifferent to misfortune unless he suffered it; contemptuous of weakness, but only identifying this in others, never in himself; a pervert without the strength of will to try to conquer his perversion . . .

Serena. Possessed of two gifts more precious than gold: inner warmth and limitless loyalty, which had first brought her happiness and then anguish, which had driven her to an act which seemed out of character unless and until one knew her well enough to understand that it was wholly in character because the stronger the loyalty, the higher the price it would demand . . .

Green had been a brilliant salesman and this had made Bennett a very wealthy man; the morality of the job had never worried Green because it was only the rich who were being swindled—he would never have helped to swindle a poor man. Then the job had come to an end because Bennett had decided to retire, careless about how his decision affected anyone else. Green's relations with his wife had never been good—he should have remembered the old Mallorquin adage, The woman you fall in love with stays behind at the altar—and when he could no longer give her enough money to satisfy her desires for suburban grandeur, they had become impossible. He'd met Serena. She was all that his wife wasn't. Their love had been intense; too intense because the gods were jealous of men and women who were too happy.

Since no individual would suffer and there was little chance at his age of his finding another really good job, he'd had no hesitation in working out a scheme to defraud the insurance company and she'd had none in agreeing to help him execute it. He was smart, so he accepted from the beginning that such a fraud had to be carried out carefully, never rushing any move, and that he must be content with a modest reward.

His plan called for a second accomplice which seemed to offer a serious weakness until one added that such an accomplice would never betray him for the good reason that to do so would inevitably result in the betrayer being, in turn, betrayed . . .

His one, fatal, mistake had been his inability fully to understand what kind of man Bennett was; just as Bennett's had been the inability to understand what kind of a man Green was. Green had failed to see that Bennett was weak as well as strong and that this weakness could lead him to believe others to be as weak as he just as his strength could incite him to act. Bennett had failed to understand that Green, who had used gentle blackmail to persuade him to help in perpetrating the fraud, would never dream of continuing to blackmail him for ever-increasing sums of money because, according to his moral values, that would have been despicable behaviour . . .

Bennett had decided that the only way to prevent his being blackmailed into poverty was to murder Green. And the proposed fraud might have been tailor-made for such a purpose. But simply to kill him after his descent by parachute would be dangerous because when questions were asked—which they certainly would be by Serena—the trail must lead straight back to him. So he had evolved a scheme which first would alert the insurance company to the fraud, secondly would confirm Green's part in the fraud and repeatedly 'prove' that he had not died in the crash, and thirdly would persuade Serena that he had gone off with another woman. (Of course, had he been able truly to appreciate Serena's character, he would have realized that she would refuse to believe this possible.)

He had set his plan in motion just before Green made his first move. In Green's name, he tried to double the capital sum assured, knowing that the insurance company would not agree immediately and that the report of Green's death so soon afterwards must automatically alert them. (Alvarez remembered how he and Ware had wondered how Green could have been so stupid and greedy as to try to double the amount just before faking his own death; they should also have wondered why he, a man with a tongue of honey, should have verbally attacked the company when they refused, rather than use all his professional charm and guile to try to talk them into doing so—one more action out of character which could have alerted them to the truth early on.)

On the afternoon of the plane crash, Bennett had set sail from Puerto Llueso in his motor-cruiser, apparently exactly following the part allotted to him in Green's plan. Yet on such a trip any reasonably smart man, however normally precise in habit, would surely have faked his log book; yet he had entered it correctly. In any ensuing investigation, details of the trip would be exposed, but this would happen as if he'd made a stupid mistake . . .

Green had rendezvoused with the motor-cruiser, set the controls of the plane, and jumped. Bennett had picked him up and they'd sailed for Stivas. But at some stage of their trip, Bennett had murdered Green and thrown his weighted body over the side. Green would never again blackmail him . . .

In Stivas, he had gone ashore and registered at the hotel in the name of Thomas Grieves (fully aware of the fact that men who changed their names used the same initials so often that it had become a presumption that the same initials meant the same person).

He'd previously armed himself with a false passport in the name of Grieves, and had not used the one Green had had with him, so there was no problem concerning the photograph. There was, of course, a risk that in the course of any inquiries by Serena, by an insurance adjuster, by the police, a photograph of Green would be shown to the hotel staff and one of them would say that it was definitely not a photograph of Grieves, but this was a risk he had weighed up and was prepared to take. He'd dyed his hair a very light brown—easy to dye it back afterwards—and had worn a false moustache—perhaps the only disguise which would not be betrayed even by sharp sunshine and one physical feature normally remembered—and he had trusted—

correctly as it turned out—that the staff of a busy hotel would be unable to remember in detail a guest they'd seen only briefly, many days before.

In the morning he'd taken a woman—presumably a prostitute, but he might have met her in other circumstances—to the hotel because if Serena made inquiries he wanted her to believe that Green had taken off with another woman and that was why he'd never returned to her. It was at this point that he'd betrayed himself, although this had not been obvious until after his own death. Prostitutes were often paid to gratify desires which other women would not. Knowing this, and inflamed by the thought, he had demanded to be whipped . . .

He'd carefully left the paperback with the fuel receipt in it in the hotel bedroom because if a really thorough investigation turned this up it would 'corroborate' the evidence of Green's fraud—never realizing that because the paperback was a crude, mildly pornographic one that featured masochism it would eventually corroborate the murder he had committed . . .

Back on the island, he'd settled down and waited to find out how his plan was working out. Before long, he'd discovered that it was not. Unknown to him at the time, two brothers out fishing had seen the parachute descend; one of them subsequently set out to blackmail him. Once again, he'd seen murder as his only way out. This time, since it could not be concealed altogether, by careful manipulation of the evidence it must be blamed on to a dead man . . . Hence the reason for first refusing to pay Carlos's blackmail demands, then volunteering to pay them—the obvious conclusion to be drawn from this must be that he could afford to defy the blackmailer but someone else, Green, could not. Hence the hiring of the car in the name of Terence Galloway, which even a casual inquiry would show to be false, and leaving it in sight outside Ca'n Feut—the obvious conclusion that the local, rather dim-witted detective must come to would be that Green had hired it and had been staying at Ca'n Feut . . .

To return to Serena. Fully conversant with Green's plan, she'd been all too easily able to judge the dangers inherent in it. And when Green failed to arrive at the flat, she must have known an ever-growing fear. Yet when Ware had spoken to her, she had had to conceal that fear and give the impression of a woman who was determined to name her lover dead even while she knew him to be alive. (And Ware had said she was not quite good enough an actress!) . . . And then Ware had told her about the woman in the hotel bedroom. Loyalty, experience, and her certainty of what kind of a man Green really was, had told her that it was quite impossible he was a masochist who had managed to keep any knowledge of this perversion from her. So the man in the hotel could not have been Green. But he had pursued Green's plan and therefore this could only mean one thing: Green was dead and the impersonator had been the murderer . . .

She was normally a person of warmth and charm; but where there was light, there was also darkness. Her emotions ran deeper, quicker, and more strongly, than most people's and so when she hated it was with a frightening intensity. The moment she suspected the terrible fact that her lover had been murdered—and this happened even as Ware spoke to her—she had determined to avenge the murder. But she had had to conceal her intention and so she had changed from a woman who knew her lover was alive, but was determined to give the impression she believed him dead, to a woman who knew he was dead but who gave the impression that she believed him to be alive even while she professed her belief in his death . . . Because how could anyone suspect her of being intent on avenging the murder of her lover if she believed him alive?

She had travelled to Mallorca and contacted Bennett in order to discover the truth. She had also met the detective in charge of the case and from him had, with the exercise of subtle charm, learned how the investigations were proceeding . . . (Had her affection been genuine or assumed? Having posed the question, Alvarez refused to try to answer it.) Eventually, she'd come to the conclusion that Bennett had covered his tracks so well that there was only one way in which she could be certain of the truth and even though this called for a course of action which filled her with a sense of repugnance, she had pursued it. She had seduced him, although he must have believed that all the moves were his, and once she was living with him had encouraged him to betray any perverted desires. And the moment he'd disclosed his masochism, she'd known beyond question that he had murdered her lover . . .

She'd poisoned one of the lunches in the deep freeze and had then left, knowing that one day the dish of pork chops in mushroom sauce would be served and she would have gained her revenge . . .

For a long time, Alvarez sat, his bitter, hopeless sadness so great it was like a physical pain. She had killed. But the man she had killed had been a murderer and therefore in her eyes her actions had been entirely justified. Yet now he, Alvarez, would be called upon to hunt her down and arrest her; that he would never, could never, do . . .

He opened the bottom right-hand drawer of the desk and brought out the bottle and a glass and poured himself out a very large brandy. When faced with an impossible, yet inescapable situation, what did a man do? If he was weak, he drank himself into a sodden state of forgetfulness, forgetting that memory must return . . .

And suddenly he realized that Bennett had inadvertently shown him that the situation was neither impossible nor inescapable. If he named Green as the murderer of Bennett, then the search would be for a man who could never be found and not for a woman who could . . . And only he could be certain that Green was not the murderer because only he knew Serena well enough . . .

The family was watching television when Alvarez walked into the room. Dolores said: 'Enrique, what has happened?'

'Nothing,' he answered dully.

'But you look terrible.'

'I'm just tired.'

'Juan, move out of that chair and let your uncle have it.'

'Why can't he sit in that one—' began Juan, pointing at a wooden-backed chair which was not only uncomfortable but also offered the worst view of the television.

'Will you kindly do as I say.'

Alvarez sat and stared blankly at the screen, seeing nothing, his mind filled with the bitterness of his sorrow. After a while the programme ended and there was a brief argument between Juan and Isabel before they left to go and play in the road. Dolores said: 'I suppose you two want feeding again?'

'Of course we do,' answered Jaime resentfully.

She stood. 'Just so long as it's not you who has to spend hours and hours in a boiling hot kitchen! Well, don't expect a feast; I'm too tired to slave much longer.' She swept through to the kitchen.

Jaime stared at Alvarez. 'It's all your bloody fault!'

'What is?'

'If you don't do something fast, we're going to become walking skeletons. We haven't had a decent meal in weeks and all because you won't let Miguel come home.'

'I've told you both, there's nothing I can do . . .' He stopped. Despite his misery, it occurred to him that circumstances had changed the situation. Carlos's murderer had suffered for his crime and that was what justice was about. On the other hand, if the murder by bombing became officially known and an investigation was launched, Miguel would be forced publicly to identify himself as a smuggler through no fault of his own and that was what injustice was about. So now it could surely only be right to let Miguel reappear and report a natural calamity at sea, cause for commiseration but not a criminal investigation . . . 'As a matter of fact, there's no reason why he shouldn't return now.'

Jaime turned towards the kitchen and shouted: 'Hey! Enrique says Miguel can return home.'

Dolores appeared in the doorway. 'And if he does, what will happen to him?'

Alvarez answered. 'Nothing, if he can think up a convincing shipwreck and rescue and his mates back him up.'

She put her hands on her hips. 'So! You have finally decided that it is after all your duty to help your own flesh and blood.'

He was too despondent to correct her.

Her tone became forgiving. 'Then perhaps, after all, I can sacrifice myself and find something a little nicer for supper.'

Alvarez was aware that a man whose heart had been broken should be totally indifferent to food, but he could not prevent himself wondering whether that 'something a little nicer' might not be lechona or even a shoulder of lamb, cooked with sage, tarragon, and garlic . . .